BRAD DUNNE'S
THE
GUT

Published in Canada by Engen Books, St. John's, NL.

Library and Archives Canada Cataloguing in Publication

Title: Brad Dunne's The Gut
Other titles: Gut
Names: Dunne, Brad, 1986- author.
Identifiers: Canadiana (print) 20200314580 | Canadiana (ebook) 20200314599 | ISBN 9781989473788
   (softcover) | ISBN 9781989473795 (PDF)
Classification: LCC PS8607.U5534 B73 2020 | DDC C813/.6—dc23

Distributed by:
Engen Books
www.engenbooks.com
submissions@engenbooks.com

First mass market paperback printing: September 2020

Cover Image: Mandi Coates
Cover Design: Jon Mercer

We acknowledge the support of ArtsNL, which last year invested $2.24 million to foster and promote the creation and enjoyment of the arts for the benefit of all Newfoundlanders and Labradorians.

NEWFOUNDLAND AND LABRADOR ARTS COUNCIL

BRAD DUNNE'S
THE GUT

ENGEN
BOOKS

CHAPTER ONE

From behind the pane of glass, Anne looked like a mermaid swimming inside a small aquarium. The light-bulb above her oscillated through different filters as a rainbow of colours shimmered along her seashell biki-ni. Her body was covered with turquoise-hued makeup shaped like scales, accented by flat-ended pearls. She tou-sled and flipped her long red hair to the beat of the house band's moody rhythm and blues jam. Through the glass she could see the shadowed outline of the man watching her. She kept her attention on his face—not the pumping action of his elbow. He had the same face they all had: a cow-like, slack-jawed rapture with a tinge of violent ag-gression in his eyes.

The band and the man both finished at the same time. Just the one song. Anne cursed to herself. At least he had the courtesy to drop the tissue into the waste basket. When he left, Anne exited the booth and went into the viewer's room. He'd left a fiver on his chair, which she tucked into her bra. She checked to make sure the paper towel dispenser was full then grabbed the waste basket to be emptied in the back room. Before she left, she briefly looked through the porthole at the trashy underwater di-orama of plastic fish dangling from dental floss and paper mache coral.

Anne went into the back room and deposited her five quid into her purse. There were enough pairs of fishnet stockings lying about to haul a quintal of cod.

"Buncha college kids tonight," Delours said.

"It's their last hurrah of the summer before buckling down for the fall semester," Anne replied. "At least the place is packed."

"They barely last one song in the peep room, sure."

"I know what you mean, honey, believe me," Anne said. "I've been doing this for ten years now and I still cringe when I step inside the booth and swallow my pride. The key is to focus on the music and let your body take over. Then it all slips away. Liban's, Temple Street, Kildare, the whole thing."

"And how long does it take for that to happen?"

"Three songs minimum."

"Seems like all I get are the one-pump chumps. How do you get your regulars?"

"You and the other greenhorns got your youth, but you haven't mastered the strut. The energy you carry is going to draw the kind of customers you want. Your vibe attracts your tribe."

A bouncer stuck his head inside. "Delours! Your turn on stage."

Delours got up to leave. Anne smiled then checked her makeup in the mirror. Another dancer approached her.

"These new girls don't know how good they got it," Marion said. "Remember when the clubs were full of gangsters and thugs? Or cops coming in expecting free-bies? And we didn't make nearly as much money back then."

"I'm not nostalgic for the old days," Anne said. "But I do miss the no-nonsense Liban's."

"You mean the floor covered in sawdust? And getting a tiny cut from serving sandwiches and watered-down beer?"

Anne laughed. "That I don't miss."

Their conversation was interrupted by the sounds of loud snorts as a few young girls ripped some lines of co-caine. Anne and Marion rolled their eyes at each other.

"They don't appreciate all this Townie cash flowing in," Marion said in a low voice. "They think this is all go-ing to last forever? I'll tell you what's going to happen. They're going to get sick of coming down here into the Gut and start setting up clubs in Baccalieu with Townie girls dancing."

"That would be the day."

"I'm telling you, we gotta start thinking about getting outta this. We're nearly thirty now."

"And go where? I can barely afford my apartment in the plateau as it is."

The bouncer stuck his head in again. "Anne! Some fel-las wanna get Ink'd!"

Anne took a sip of water then headed out.

The Townies lining the bar wore squids atop their heads, the long tentacles pouring over their shoulders and the mantles forming little steeples. She could tell by their youthful wide eyes that this was their first time in a Kil-dare strip club. Anne poured each of them a shot of Ink. After a quick flourish with her lighter, she set each glass alight. Blue flames flickered from the tiny pools of hard black rum.

"Hold your glasses high!" she commanded.

The men obeyed.

Everyone in the bar, including the band, was silent while Anne attended to the ritual.

"You Townies may kiss the cod in Baccalieu, but in the Gut we smooch the squid. And if it's the blessings of Kildare ye seek, then repeat after me, '*Mo sheacht mbeannacht ort!*'"

The Townies did their best imitation: "Muh hyawcht mann-acht urt!"

"Now drink!" Anne announced.

They blew out the flame then shot back their Ink. Anne relished the looks of surprised delight in their faces as they registered the medley of caramelized sugars and vanilla revealed by the fire. They slid her some tips, which she tucked into her seashell bra.

Póg Mo Thóin took to the stage with their matching mid-length hairstyles to resume their eight-hour set. Delours stepped back on stage and danced to their rhythm and blues jam. She was even on beat. Her make-up was a little overboard, like she'd just been dragged from the Gut and pulled on stage. Anne was going to have to give her a tutorial on that. Customers wanted fantasy not verisimilitude.

A young man gently tapped Anne's elbow. He looked like most any of the other Townie college kids: dark complexion pocked with the vestiges of acne, some nascent facial hair, and a rapid vacillation between arrogance and insecurity. All Anne cared to see was the colour of money.

"Can I have a dance?" he asked.

She curled her fingers around his and led him to the booths. Before she let him in, she placed a finger on his chest and looked him directly in the eyes.

"Five bucks a song, sweetie," she said.

He nodded quickly.

This one lasted four songs.

And so the night went—just like every other night nowadays. A peep show, followed by an Inking, followed by another peep show. The band kept playing and the roll of bills in her purse expanded.

Soon after last call, the men left the club to make their way either to the brothels or back to Baccalieu. Anne went to the back room to change. The seashell lingerie and platform shoes were replaced by joggers and flip-flops. She didn't bother to completely wipe away all the makeup—she would take a long, hot shower back at her apartment. With her tousled crimson hair tied up into a sloppy ponytail, she left Liban's.

It was a typically mauzy late-summer night. Drunk men and women slipped on the slick cobblestones of Temple Street. Above Liban's doorway was a flashing neon sign of animated hands groping a mermaid. As she stepped out, it shut off for the night. A sharp breeze cut through the sticky heat, hinting at the oncoming fall. It carried with it a thick waft of fish guts from the Gut. Anne's perfume battled hard against the bouquet of brine, offal, and whatever else was dumped into the harbour.

A troupe of drunken Townies stumbling around outside the club recognized her. The sweats and flip-flops did little to dissuade their attentions.

"Aye, me lassie," one bellowed at her in an exaggerated imitation of a Kildare accent. "How much to wrap yer arms around me like a squid and kiss me cod?"

Anne recognized the harasser as one of the Townie college kids she'd given a peep show earlier. Within the booth, she was an object of desire, perhaps even worship. But now that they were outside of her territory, he needed to demean her, put her in her place in front of his boys.

She knew that the bouncers weren't about to throw down for a girl outside the confines of their club, especially against Townies, so she turned around and walked the other way, head down, scanning the street for a cab. The Townies continued to follow her, their catcalls becoming more feral, more obscene. She heard their footsteps getting closer, their voices louder, could almost smell the drunkenness on their breaths. A cop car briefly flashed its lights and pulled up to the side of the road. Anne's brief sense of cautious optimism evaporated when she looked inside and saw that the officers were both Townies themselves. The passenger side window rolled down and one of the young officers poked his head out.

"I hope you boys aren't giving this young lady a hard time," he said with a smirk.

"No, sir," one of the gang announced.

"Alright, lads," the officer said. "Keep it civil." He rolled up his window and they drove on.

When the car was out of sight, Anne could see the grins on the lads emboldened. She turned quickly and walked faster.

"Hey, you Merfie cunt," one of the boys shouted at her. "We're just trying to make you some money."

His buddies tried to play it off and calm him down, but the word "Merfie" drew the attention of some Merrow boys walking up the street.

"Why don't you Townies fuck off back to Baccalieu," one of the Merrow boys yelled.

With that came the usual dance of overtly masculine posturing, which quickly escalated into a street fight. The cops returned. They got out of their cars and each grabbed a local boy. The others ran away. The Townies stood around watching, laughing. Anne took the distraction as an opportunity to hurry around the corner onto another street. A large black coupe pulled up beside her. The tires' rubber caressed the dimples of the cobblestone street. Anne glanced over and saw the gold spokes of the rims, which were the size of bicycle wheels, and a tiny statue of a mermaid atop the front of the hood. Likely a rich john from Baccalieu looking for something she didn't sell. She kept walking. The car's window rolled down.

"Boys will be boys," a woman's voice said.

Anne stopped. First, because she'd never heard tell of a woman driving a car, let alone one as fancy as this one. Second, because she recognized the voice.

"Patricia?" she said. "Is that you?"

"Indeed, it is."

"I haven't seen you in ages. We all thought you joined the convent or something."

Patricia laughed. "Something like that. Why don't you hop in and I'll tell you all about it. Looks like you could use a ride right now."

Anne got in the passenger side, the leather seat crinkling beneath her. Patricia was wearing a long green trench coat and a pair of culottes below. Certainly a modest shift from when they used to work together in the clubs not too long ago. Patricia drove down the street and they could see the cops talking to the Townies while two local boys sat in the back of their car.

Patricia sighed. "Typical."

"I was lucky our boys showed up," Anne said. "Those Townies were about to get out of hand. And it's not like the cops were about to do anything about it."

"Oh, I know," Patricia replied. "That's the way our society works. There must be in-groups whom the law protects but does not bind, alongside out-groups whom the law binds but does not protect."

Anne mulled this over. It sounded like something her brother would say.

"It must be five years since we last saw each other," Anne said.

"That's right. Not long after Colleen was murdered.

Anne shifted in her seat. "Where did you get this car?"

"First, let me ask you something," Patricia replied. "Aren't you tired of putting on that ridiculous outfit to get a few dollars from Townies?"

"It's not so bad. Beats waitressing."

"It's debasing. We dress up like mermaids to fulfill a racist fantasy. It all stems from when the Indesejável first arrived on our shore. We didn't share their puritanical views on sex and were happy to exchange it for whatever tools or trinkets they had to trade. In their misunderstanding, they believed the Merrow were only good for fishing and fucking."

Anne was taken aback again. Calling Townies 'Indesejável' and Merfies 'Merrow' seemed very formal for Patricia.

"But that's how the game works. When men come from Baccalieu to the Gut they expect to see merfolk. You got to give the customer what they want."

"But you don't give them everything they want, do you?"

Patricia navigated the empty streets of downtown Kildare with an expertise only a local was capable of. Kildare was a confusing network of one-way streets—until recently used exclusively by horse and carriage—rippling out from the Gut like a spider's web. A few drunks stumbled around looking for a cab, but quickly got out of the way of the car when they saw the money it represented. She drove past the row houses of downtown Kildare and up into the residential hills of the plateau. Anne looked out over the dimly lit bowl of wood and stone surrounding the Gut, which abruptly gave way to the radiant sprawl of Baccalieu.

"I don't turn tricks like some of the other girls," Anne said. "But I'm not going to judge anyone for it."

"Of course," Patricia answered. "I don't judge anyone in Kildare doing whatever they can to make money, either. Especially if they're not hurting anyone doing it. I just think we're capable of more. And we deserve it. I'm sick of people like us having to accept the terms set down by the colonizers just to get by. This place belongs to us."

"You sound like my brother," Anne replied. "I hear what you're saying, but what are we supposed to do?"

"I'm glad you asked me that. The last few years, I've

been a part of a group whose mission has been to get Kildare back to its former glory and allow the people who live here to flourish. Merrow like us."

"That sounds really great," Anne said. "I'm happy for you."

They pulled up outside the Davis Flats apartment complex.

"How did you know I lived here?" Anne asked.

"Oh, you mentioned it earlier," Patricia said.

Anne was about to get out when Patricia grabbed her arm.

"Do you want to see what I'm talking about?"

"What, like, right now?"

"Yes."

Anne hesitated. "I don't know," she said.

Patricia stared directly into her eyes with a soft intensity. Her green eyes radiated in the darkness. A yellow ring formed around her pupils and swelled into her irises. Anne was transfixed by this play of colours. She could feel the pressure of Patricia's gaze, reaching into her heart with her eyes and studying all her secrets—and she welcomed it.

"I know you, Anne," Patricia continued. "I know that you're a hard worker, with a good heart, and a good head on your shoulders. Like so many of us, you could achieve great things if only you were given the opportunity. And I know you see it inside yourself, too." She let go off Anne's arm. "After Colleen was murdered, I really lost hope. I couldn't deal with it anymore. I blamed myself, I blamed us, Merrow, for our crime and gangs and drugs and violence and murders. But then I realized that was bullshit, too. It was a bullshit narrative the colonizers sold to us and we believed it. Obviously, we're not above crime as a race. There will always be criminals. But we can break the cycle of violence by breaking the systematic injustice the colonizers have thrust upon us for hundreds of years. I want my brothers and sisters to enjoy the same prosperity as the Townies. No more tricking, dancing, serving, slinging. And no more Colleens."

Through Patricia's eyes, Anne scurried through Davis Flats' corridors, ramps, and stairwells like a rat trapped in a maze. Her one-bedroom burrow was squeezed between screaming children, crying women, and angry drunken men, separated by cheap, thin walls. But the ceiling was hard ceiling, too hard for her to break through alone. Her nights, past, present, and future, spread out before her like a row of empty shot glasses. She was going to break the ceiling.

"OK," she said. "Let's go."

Patricia drove through the plateau and onto the highway that brought them up into the hills. The trees eventually gave way to the massive properties of rich Townies who migrated there to build their tacky mansions. Patricia slowed and turned onto a long driveway that led to a gate. A couple of guys, who held themselves with the posture Anne recognized as corner boys, opened it. They drove down another long driveway. Between the trees and in the darkness, Anne could see glittering lamps hinting at the size of a colossal estate. The treeline broke and what should have been a view over the whole bay area was dominated by the mansion. Anne couldn't determine its colour or style other than it was big and dark and towering over her, like it was growing out of the ground. Its enormity was baffling. From every angle she considered, the house seemed to stretch to fill the space.

"Impressive, isn't it?" Patricia asked. "It's called Talamh an Eisc."

Anne nodded. It was indeed a beautiful mansion.

Patricia pulled into a multi-car garage beside a lush courtyard. More hard-looking men patrolled the grounds. At the front of the mansion, a row of white columns supported a balcony. Patricia led Anne through them to a large oak door like they were entering the mouth of a giant monster. The handle was iron wrought into a squid's tentacle.

"Don't be intimidated," Patricia said with a smile. "By the way, people call me Boudica around here. But you can still call me Patricia in private."

CHAPTER TWO

Kieran awoke to the sound of knocking at his door. Maeve was still asleep beside him. He slipped out of bed and crept down the hall on the balls of his feet. A quick glance into Aoife's room confirmed that his daughter was still asleep in her crib. He shuffled down the staircase, the wood creaking gently under his size. There was another quick knock at his door.

"Hold on, hold on," he whispered.

Kieran swung the door open and found Ms. Conway with her finger inches away from the doorbell. He gave her as stern a glare as he could muster for the old woman.

"I'm sorry to bother you like this, Kier," she pleaded. "But it's them two. They're at it again. Real bad this time. I'm afraid he's gonna hurt her."

"Don't worry about it, Ms. Conway," he replied. "Let me get some shoes on and I'll be right behind you."

Kieran grabbed a flashlight and a coat then slipped his bare feet into a pair of shoes. The night air nipped at the ankles left exposed beneath his pyjamas. He followed Ms. Conway a few streets over. A small audience had formed outside of Connor and Molly's row house. Kieran could hear screaming and shouting coming from inside. Something made contact with glass and smashed it. The crowd gasped. Kieran marched up to the door and knocked firmly.

"What the fuck do you want?" Connor yelled from inside.

"Open this door before I knock it down," Kieran replied.

Angry footsteps stomped towards the door. It swung opened wildly. The hostility in Connor's face softened when he laid eyes on Kieran's 6'5" frame filling the doorway.

"I'm sorry, Kier-K-Officer-Detective Hynes," he said. "We didn't mean to be causing a racket."

"Molly!" Kieran called out.

The skinny woman eventually came to the door. Kieran turned on his flashlight and looked the two hell raisers up and down. They swayed gently while trying to stand straight. Molly's eyes were puffy and swollen from crying, but she didn't appear to have any marks on her.

"I want to talk to you alone," Kieran said. He looked at Connor and gestured his head towards the couch. Connor obeyed.

"What's going on?" Kieran asked Molly.

"It was just a little argument that got out of hand," she said, her voice was slurred as Connor's. "It's over now. It's fine. Really."

"You know I can take you to a shelter whenever you want. Just say the word."

She looked down at her feet and swayed towards Kieran then backwards.

"We're fine," she said, loud enough for Connor to hear. "Tell everyone we're sorry."

"You won't hear boo from us any more tonight," Connor called out. "I promise."

Kieran looked behind Molly at the smashed mirror. A cracked ceramic pot lay beneath, green leaves and brown dirt scoured on the carpet. He considered his reflection: a crooked nose and cauliflower ears. The fractured image collapsed his wide clavicles making him appear slight and squat.

Kieran turned off his flashlight and walked away. Molly shut the door behind him.

"Show's over!" he announced. "Everyone can go home."

The crowd slowly dissipated, murmuring their disappointment.

"Can't you do more?" Ms. Conway asked. "He's always beating her. Everyone knows it. I mean, she's no angel herself, but surely something can be done to help her."

"Unfortunately, there's not much we can do unless she files a report."

Ms. Conway shook her head. "Thanks anyway."

"Any time."

Kieran walked back to his house. He trudged up the stairs to his room and was about to get back into bed when he saw on his clock that it was 4:15 a.m.

"More time for a lazy breakfast," he sighed to himself and switched off his 5 a.m. alarm.

Maeve stirred at the sound of his voice. He bent down and pushed her red curly hair aside to lay a soft kiss on her freckled cheek. A little sleepy grin broke across her face and she cuddled into the pillows and fell back to sleep. Kieran went downstairs and put on a big pot of coffee. While that brewed, he fried some eggs and bologna, which he liked with plenty of mustard, and made some toast, which he liked with plenty of butter. The coffee was finished, and he poured himself a large mugful with no milk or sugar. After breakfast, he went to his office and ironed his pants. He put on his white collared shirt and tied a half Windsor around his neck. On his desk was a picture of his university rugby squad. He picked it up and looked at it, downing the last of his coffee. Even in black and white it was clear that he was the only Merrow on the team.

The sun was peeking out over the horizon, filling the windows with soft light. Just as he was going out the front door, he heard Aoife cry. He gently closed the door and got into the car. A smirk broke out across as his face as he saw the light in the bedroom switch on. Many of his neighbours were also leaving their homes as the plateau's middle class began their day. Kieran made his way towards the Baccalieu Area Police Department precinct in downtown Kildare.

"Earlier than usual," Detective McCrae said when he saw Kieran enter the office. "Even for you."

"I figured I'd come in and make sure you weren't asleep."

"You should know better than anyone that a Merfie can't afford the luxury of napping on the night shift."

"Neighbour woke me up to help settle a domestic disturbance."

"Let me guess. Connor and Molly? Did you finally stick his dick in the dirt?"

"I tried to deal with it as a neighbour, not a cop."

"People like that are hopeless. All they understand is this." McCrae held up meaty fist. "Speaking of which, I have a present for you."

"Sorry, I forgot it was our anniversary."

"I won't hold it against you. Your red ball on Bally-bane? The one with the stepfather beaten to death? Stepson in the wind? Well, guess what. Patrol brought him in last night. Something about petty theft, trying to jack up a Townie buying heroin. The kid gave a fake name, but I recognized him. He's in the cooler now. Been there a couple hours."

"Damn, that is a nice present. Now I feel bad I didn't get you anything."

"I'm just glad you're back from consulting on the case on the east side of Baccalieu. Is it true that you asked the Deputy of Operations to leave the crime scene? And he listened?"

"Guy was talking too loud," Kieran smirked. "I couldn't think clearly."

"The balls on you. Maeve is a lucky woman."

"Did you take his fingerprint yet?"

"Yeah but we won't be able to get a match on the murder weapon until the guys get into the lab. We won't get that back until the afternoon, minimum."

"Our friend doesn't know that."

McCrae laughed. "Balls on ya! Hey, your partner has arrived."

Detective Martim Santiago arrived with a cup of coffee in one hand, a cigarette in the other, and dark bags under his eyes. He consumed the caffeine and nicotine as if they would give him another couple hours of sleep.

"How's he doing?" McCrae asked.

"Not bad," Kieran replied. "What he lacks in smarts he makes up for in hard work. He's certainly giving these early mornings his best. I got this. You take off for the day."

McCrae left and Santiago now stood in his place.

"We have our suspect for the Heaney case," Kieran said.

"The stepson?"

"Yeah, he's in the cooler now. I'm going to handle this one solo. You watch through the mirror."

"Got it. How you gonna play it? Strict father or big brother? A little bit of both?"

"I think I'll freestyle it. Been listening to a lot of jazz lately."

Kieran left Santiago with a confused look on his face. He grabbed a file from his desk then entered the interrogation room. A skinny, freckled kid sat at the table. He recognized Kieran. His cheeks turned beet red and he looked down at the shackles around his wrists.

"Jaime?" Kieran asked.

The kid looked up then back down immediately. "That's not my name."

"What was the name you gave the officer who arrested you?"

"Patrick. Patrick Sullivan. Because that's my real name."

"Right."

Kieran leaned over and unshackled the kid. Jaime/Patrick massaged his wrists. He looked at the wooden table and seemed to notice the scrapes and dents for the first time. Kieran laid the folder atop the table and sat across from the kid.

"So, you're here because you tried to mug a Townie?"

"The guy was a junkie. They didn't even take him for trying to buy heroin."

"How old are you, Jaime?"

"Eighteen. And that's not my name."

Kieran smiled. "Too old to go back to Agueda either way."

Panic seized the kid's face.

"I know you've done time there, Jaime," Kieran said. No denial this time. "And I know what happens to some of the kids there." He let that sit for a minute. The kid was shaking.

"Did they make you fight?" Kieran asked.

"Yeah. And I never lost. That's why..."

"That's why the counsellors never tried anything with you?"

"That's right! They wouldn't fuck with me. Some of the other boys, though. No one ever believed me when I told them about what really goes on there."

"I believe you. I know all about it. And I believe that they never laid their hands on you. Because you're tough. And they could see, like I can, that no one was going to fuck with you without a fight."

Jaime nodded his head and wiped away tears from his eyes.

"You know what else I know? I know that your stepdad was a creep just like those counsellors. And, sure, he wasn't going to go after you, but your little brother isn't as tough as you, is he?"

The table rocked as Jaime's shoulders shook. He didn't try to fight back the tears now. Kieran stood up and brought his chair near to him.

"No," Jaime said. "That wasn't me. I don't know what you're talking about."

"You know those smudges the officers took of your fingers when you got here?" Jaime looked at his hands and considered the ink on his fingertips. "Well we have guys who matched your fingerprints to the hurling club you used to beat your stepfather to death." Jaime was pale. He tried to open his mouth to speak, but he just gulped like a fish out of water. "I'm sorry to be the one to tell you this, but your mom gave you up. She still loved that bastard no matter what he did to your little brother. Now, with her testimony and the forensic evidence, we got enough to put you away. Except, this time, you're going to Cadeia as an adult. General population. And believe me, whatever you experienced at Agueda is going to seem like a dream compared to Cadeia."

"No! It's not fair! He was fucking around with Jason. I had to stop him. I didn't want to kill him, but we started to fight and it just got out of hand."

"It's OK. I get it. Believe me. Frankly, between you and me, you did this town a big favour. I got no sympathy for creeps who mess with kids. And you know who else doesn't? Judges and juries."

Jaime started to relax a bit. "It was self-defence anyway, right?"

"Sounds like it to me. But, I'm not a lawyer. I'm just a

cop who needs to get your side of it. Can you do that?"

Jaime nodded. Kieran opened up the folder and passed a pen and paper to Jaime.

"This is a contract that acknowledges your confession. It waives your right to remain silent."

"I'm not really great at reading and writing."

"Can you sign your name? Just sign at the bottom and then I'll write down everything you say."

Two hours later, Kieran emerged from the interrogation room with a sore hand and a written confession. He sat down to his desk to review his document. Two officers escorted Jaime out of the interrogation room to processing.

"That was masterful," Santiago told Kieran. "The way you played the waiver? Perfection."

"I told you," Kieran replied. "Jazz."

"Right. Guess I'll have to start listening to that."

"It's about using the tools that are available to you and trusting your instincts. You have to find your own rhythm in there. No two detectives will interrogate a suspect the same way. It's an art."

"He recognized you as soon as you walked in. It's crazy how these kids from the Gut look up to you."

Kieran laughed. "Some of them. Most of them hate me."

"I'd say they're jealous. First Merrow from Kildare to get a full athletic scholarship to Baccalieu University as the star rugby player. I don't have anything like that going for me."

"Sure you do. A lot of these guys are intimidated by the power you represent. They'll put on a tough guy act, but that's just to hide their fear. You'll get there eventually."

"Hynes!" Cardosa called out.

"Yes, Major," Kieran replied.

"There's a Sean Gallagher here to see you. Missing sister."

"Send him over."

"You don't mean the same..." Santiago asked.

"Here." Kieran handed Santiago the confession. "Type this up for me, will you?"

The whole office quieted as Gallagher, dressed in professorial tweed, approached Kieran's desk. Gallagher's stoic face didn't betray any sense of anxiety or resentment.

"Good to see you, Dr. Gallager," Kieran said.

"Please, call me Sean."

"It's been awhile."

"Yes. Five years."

"Alright, Sean. Take a seat. The Lieutenant tells me your sister is missing?"

"Yes. Anne."

"How long?"

"About a month now."

Kieran pulled open a drawer from his desk and retrieved a sand-coloured notebook. He cracked it open and began jotting down a few notes. He looked up and saw Sean staring at the stack of similar notebooks on his desk. Detectives, officers, and clerical workers passed by Kieran's desk, barely bothering to conceal their eavesdropping.

"I feel like getting some coffee," Kieran said. "How

about you?"

"Um, well, I guess..."

"Great. There's a spot just down the street that's a hel-luva lot more drinkable than the engine grease we drink here."

Sean followed Kieran out of the precinct under the dis-appointed glances of their eavesdroppers. They went into O'Grady's Diner and sat across from each other on vinyl-covered seats at a Formica table. A waitress came and took their orders. The special of the day was clam chowder. Both ordered just black coffee. Kieran considered Sean's starched collar and perfect half Windsor knot.

"I see our lessons from boarding school haven't left you either," Kieran observed.

"Demerits for any slack tie, untucked shirt, or blem-ished shoe," Sean said. "They never cut us Merrow any slack."

The waitress laid two coffee mugs between them.

"There's no way to stop tongues from wagging in the Gut," Kieran said, "but I figured we'd be better off at least getting out of the precinct office."

"Fair enough."

"Tell me about Anne."

"We're not really close, but I do call about once a week to check in on her. And for the last month or so, I haven't been able to reach her. I went by her apartment in the pla-teau a few times and no one seems to be there. I asked some of her neighbours and they haven't seen her either." He picked up his cup with a trembling hand. "I can't lose another sister."

"Does she dance?"

Sean hesitated and took a sip of coffee. "Yes."

"The reason I ask is because we've had a string of similar disappearances."

"I thought as much when I saw the pile of notebooks on your desk."

"I'm going to level with you here. And I'm telling you this because I feel like I owe you one after what went down with Colleen." Sean flinched at the mention of her name. "There's some weird shit going down in Kildare. These missing persons cases keep piling up, but because there's no bodies there's no real sense of urgency around the department. We're talking about a district with less than 200,000 people and over one hundred homicides a year. I'm trying to get more resources, but no one wants to hear about it. Legally, as far as they're concerned: no body, no crime."

"I'm sure the fact that they're Merrow has a lot to do with that," Sean said.

It was Kieran's turn to flinch.

"My biggest challenge is that most missing persons are female and so are the potential witnesses," he explained. "They work at bars, clubs, and brothels. I can't get them to open up to me. They're all too spooked."

"What about your old partner," Sean asked. "Maria Costa."

Kieran sighed. "She's not on the force anymore. But here's the thing: She's gone private."

"Like a private investigator?"

"Yes, exactly."

"So, what are you suggesting?"

"That you reach out to her. Get her to take your case.

She'll blow this whole thing wide open. I know it."

They both sipped their coffees.

"OK," Sean said. "I'll do it. How do I contact her?"

Kieran took out his wallet and pulled out a business card. Before he handed it to Sean, he said: "There's a hitch. I've been trying to hire her myself on behalf of the department, but she's refused."

"What's the issue?"

"Everything that happened with Colleen really messed her up. That's when she quit the force." He slid the card across the table to Sean then stood up. "But my instincts tell me you're the fulcrum I've been waiting for."

CHAPTER THREE

Maria sat at her desk, smoking another cigarette, listening to another version of the same story she'd heard countless times over the last five years. When she first started out as a private investigator, word must have gotten around quickly during brunch with mimosas that Maria Costa was the one to hire if you suspected your husband was two-timing.

"For the last few months, I've been able to smell perfume on his suits when he comes home late," Ms. Almeida said. "I think he's going to the whorehouses in the Gut. Sticking his shrimp dick inside those Merfie cunts. Bringing home who knows what kind of disease. I'm afraid to go to the doctor."

Ms. Almeida was still relatively young, transitioning from a pretty young lady to a beautiful woman. But beautiful women have a harder time getting husbands than their younger counterparts. Maria was guessing Ms. Almeida wanted to cut her losses on this marriage while she still had some skin in the game. The fact that she came here herself instead of through the lawyer told Maria that Mr. Almeida was the money. But she was surprised at how personally Ms. Almeida was taking this betrayal. Perhaps she actually loved Mr. Almeida. Most likely, though, it was wounded pride talking. Whatever the case, Maria was sick of inhaling Ms. Almeida's filtered cigarettes, which tasted like fog strained through cotton wool.

"I'll take your case," she said, interrupting the soon-to-be bachelorette. "Speak to my secretary about payment details."

"Thank you," Ms. Almeida said and promptly left the office.

Maria stood up and went over to her window over-looking the Baccalieu harbour. The afternoon was wind-ing down and people were leaving their offices. Some were coming to the street-level bistro of her building—her father's building. She took a deep drag from her un-filtered cigarette and cursed her personal rule of banning booze from the office.

When she heard Ms. Almeida leave, she closed up for the day. Before leaving, she grabbed a bag with some plain clothes and a camera. In the foyer, her secretary in-tercepted her before she could hurry out the door.

"I got another call from Kieran Hynes today," Ms. Nunes said. "I can't keep putting him off."

"Deal with him," Maria said. She flipped the sign from OPEN to CLOSED against the frosted glass. "That's what I pay you for."

She left and shut the door. Written on the outside of the glass:

Maria Costa

Private Investigator

It was around 5 p.m. and traffic in the city centre was cramped. Taxis weren't stopping and Maria shuddered at the idea of squeezing into a packed streetcar. The walk to Peixe was only a few blocks anyway. The docks at the harbour teemed with people vying at the market. Gulls circled around the fish processing plant, snatching pieces of guts, gills, and cartilage. The rich smell of salted cod mingled with the sickly-sweet stink of gasoline dripping from the trawlers and cargo ships. Underneath it was the pungent odour of the harbour. Apparently, the water could be used to develop film. Maria was often tempted to try it as a cost-saving measure. Her mother liked to talk about the days before the wooden longliners gave way to steel, and when the wharves and flakes were replaced by concrete docks and fish plants. Everything seemed to be simpler then, more pure—even though most of the old crowd, like her mother, looked down on Kildare where the Gut was still mostly wood.

Peixe was nestled in that sweet spot of King's Boulevard where it was away from the stench of the harbour, but not too far north where it was mostly residential and thus unfashionable. The creative class had managed to carve out a niche in Baccalieu and filled it with restaurants, cafes, and studios. Downtown Baccalieu's severe aesthetic was a testament to the grim settlers who'd colonized the bay. Sharing at least this much with her ancestors, Maria could care less about beautification. As long as there were plenty of bodegas to get whiskey, smokes, and the occasional fish and chips, she was satisfied.

Maria went around to the alleyway and knocked on the staff door. A tall man with thick, hairy forearms and a barrel of a stomach answered.

"Maria!" Aloisio exclaimed and pulled her inside. "You must try this soup I'm perfecting."

She had little choice as he guided her through the busy kitchen. A frenetic staff was busy preparing for the evening's service. Chefs and porters scurried around in a controlled chaos amidst the melange of scents. Aloisio led her over to a great pot. He held up a ladle, which Maria gladly slurped. Its savoury flavour rolled her eyes into the back of her head.

"It's my newest caldeirada," Aloisio explained. "You like?"

"It's delicious," Maria said. She held up her hand and interjected before Aloisio could launch into a twenty-minute exposition on his fish stew and how it was a clever modern update of his mother's recipe. "What about that guest I was asking you about?"

"Ah. Of course. It is indeed him, as you said. He doesn't even bother to come with a fake name when making a reservation with his mistress. He'll be here tonight at 8 p.m."

"Excellent. Think you could get me on the list?"

"For you? Anything. I'll have my staff set you up at the bar."

"Thanks, Aloisio," she said. "Please give my regards to Ines. I'm going to leave my bag in your office. I'll get it later."

"Wait. Please take some with you." Without giving Maria the option of refusing, he began filling up a thermos with caldeirada and thrust it into her hands. "You're far too skinny and you look tired. You work too hard."

Maria indulged these avuncular familiarities with an exaggerated eye roll. She left the restaurant. Traffic was flowing a bit more freely now. She hopped on a streetcar and found a seat where she was sure not to brush shoulders with anyone. The streetcars' cables crisscrossed at intersections, forming giant steel nets. As it travelled westward, white collar suits and ties turned into blue collar jeans and t-shirts. Well-manicured green spaces dwindled, and trash heaps multiplied. Pediments held up by stone columns were replaced by cracked stoops. Maria's apartment building was at the last stop. Before going up to her one-room apartment, she grabbed a pack of cigarettes from the street-level bodega. The husband and wife who ran the shop usually just exchanged a friendly nod as opposed to inane small talk, which Maria appreciated.

In the lobby, an older lady was getting into the elevator. Maria hung back and waited until she went in. Once it was empty, she pulled open the scissor gate and punched in her floor number before anyone could try and join her. The elevator brought her up to her floor. The superintendent was vacuuming the dull red carpet of the hallway. Maria tread softly under the cover of the vacuum's hum and made her way to her apartment without being detected.

She laid the thermos on her otherwise empty kitchen table, aside from a bottle of whiskey, and went to the cupboards. Her only bowl was a little dusty, so she rinsed it out and emptied the caldeirada into it. She sat down on her couch and turned on the radio, set to her favourite jazz station. Aloisio had really outdone himself with this one. The soup was a perfect balance of lean and oily fish with cod and mackerel—although Maria would prefer octopus over mackerel, but a restaurant in Baccalieu would never do that. The potatoes, peppers, onions, and tomatoes were infused with the broth's spices and brine. The soup, the whiskey, and the music worked together to ease her shoulders. She felt the strains in her neck slowly yield. When her bowl was empty, she lit a cigarette and thought about how nice it would be to just sit on the couch for the rest of the evening, listening to music and smoking. But she had work to do, so she rubbed the cigarette out in the ashtray, grabbed the bottle of whiskey, and headed to the bathroom for a shower.

Getting ready was made easy by the fact that she only had one cocktail dress and one pair of heels. Not only did the dress and shoes make her feel uncomfortable, she also didn't like having her long wavy hair pouring over her shoulders. The only reason she kept her hair long was for nights like tonight. Once her makeup was finished, she looked in the mirror and got into character. First, she eased her brow then retracted her defiant chin. Once her resting-bitch-face was gone, she worked on practising her smile and laugh. She was drunk enough not to feel repulsed. With her mask ready and her buzz good and tight, she went outside to fetch a cab. Men gazed at her longer than usual. And when the first cab immediately pulled up to the curve, she knew that she was on her game.

"Peixe," she said when she got into the back of the cab.

"Right away, ma'am," the cabbie said in a Merfie accent. She could see red hair sticking out from underneath his cap.

Behind them, she noticed a cab pull out with its on-duty sign turned off. It did a piss poor job of prairie dogging them all the way downtown. Maria thought to suggest to her cabbie to take a different route and throw off the trail, but, not feeling threatened by the amateurism, she was curious to see who was following them. She got out by Peixe and paid the cabbie. The other cab drove by without Maria getting a good look at who was in the backseat.

The restaurant was full, as usual. Maria recognized a lot of the local power players: Mafiosos and politicians and businessmen who operated somewhere between those two worlds. She went to the head of the line, gave the hostess her name, and was led over to the bar which gave her a nice vantage point of Councilman Gaetan Ferreira and his date for the evening.

Philandering men came in a variety of flavours: weekend warriors who couldn't handle their recreational substances; easily manipulated mopes who fell in love with their secretaries; skirt-chasers who'd stick their dick in a bowl of soup if it was still warm. Then there were rare breeds like Councilman Ferreira. He wasn't just cheating on his wife for pleasure — it was business too. To show up at a swanky restaurant like Peixe with a beautiful mistress was a demonstration of power. He wanted to be seen, to show everyone what he was capable of getting away with.

Maria was about to order something when a man came over and sat beside her.

"Can I buy you a drink?" he asked.

"Of course," she said and smiled at this foolish little fly that had wandered into her web. "Glass of Shiraz, please."

Aside from having to dress the part, going undercover also often required sacrificing whiskey.

Ferreira's date looked across the restaurant to the bar where Maria was sitting and made eye contact. Maria frowned and the escort quickly re-directed her attention back to Ferreira. Curious, he turned around to see what had caught his date's attention. Maria kept her attention on her suitor. She cursed the escort; she'd specifically instructed her not to look for her when she recruited her for this job. At least she'd only paid half up front.

This swinging dick buying her drinks was actually quite charming and could gamely return her flirty volleys. He was a typical upper-middle class Townie with ambitions of penthouses and platinum credit cards. Something about investment banking or whatever. The nice thing about these aggressive ladder climbers is they cut to the chase and quickly vanished the morning after when they realized what part of the neighbourhood they'd woken up in. She played with him the way a cat played with a mouse, all the while keeping Councilman Ferreira in her peripheral. When she saw him request the bill, she stood up.

"Bathroom?" her suitor asked, his confidence betrayed by a hint of anxiety.

"Sorry," she said. "Have to go." She took a quick appraisal of his jawline then pulled over a napkin and snatched a pen from behind the bar. After scribbling her number down, she thrust it at him. "Here. Call me in about two hours if you're still keen."

She walked towards the bathrooms then ducked into the kitchen. Aloisio was shouting orders at his staff, too much in the flow of his work to notice Maria. She grabbed her bag of clothes that she'd left in his office and changed quickly. Happy to be out of her dress and heels, she stuffed them into the bag beside the camera then tied her hair back with an elastic. A few of the staff out having a smoke break in the alley eyed her briefly with curiosity as she darted out to the busy boulevard. She saw Ferreira and his date get into a cab. Maria cut off some people to hop in the next available one.

"You can't do that," the cabbie protested, another Merfie.

"I'll pay you double if you follow that cab ahead of us," she offered.

He shut up and took off. Fortunately, this guy was better at prairie dogging than whoever had been following her earlier. Maria knew where Ferreira was going, but she didn't want to take the chance that he'd change up at the last minute and blow her chance. They followed the councilman and his mistress westward to a cheap hotel near the unofficial border between Baccalieu and Kildare. Maria was a little disappointed by this. Up until now, Ferreira had eschewed many of his peers' stereotypes. This gutter trash wish fulfillment was such a cliché. At least she wouldn't have to go far to get back to her apartment.

After Ferreira checked in and went up the elevator, Maria went over to the porter.

"I booked them in the room you requested," he said.

Maria gave him his tip and went out and into the adjacent alleyway. She climbed up the fire escape ladder and settled into her vantage point. From her backpack she grabbed her camera and trained the zoom. Ferreira went to the window to shut the blinds, but his date pulled him over to the bed before he got the chance. *Good girl*, Maria thought. She might as well have been shooting a nature documentary.

After she descended the staircase and got back onto the street, she heard some clumsy footsteps approaching her quickly. Absorbed in the hunt, and a little drunk, she'd forgotten that someone had been hunting her tonight as well. She pulled a telescopic baton from her bag, spun around, and swung it downwards. The attacker grabbed his knee and collapsed to the ground, which gave her a chance to fish out her brass knuckles. When he stood up and charged, she was ready. A well-placed right hook to his jaw brought him down again. Now it was time for the switchblade. She pushed the creep up against the wall and held the knife to his throat.

"Who are you?" she asked. "What do you want?"

"Ruining someone else's life tonight, eh?" he answered and spit out a wad of blood and teeth.

His once handsome features were now mostly eroded, but Maria recognized the gaunt and pocked face as Joao Oliveira. She'd helped his wife empty his savings during their divorce proceedings thanks to some pictures she'd taken of him with his secretary. The knife pricked his skin a little and drew a trickle of blood. She pulled it away then drove her knee into his crotch. He collapsed on the ground, writhing in pain, breathing sharply through his broken teeth.

"You took everything from me, you bitch!" he barked.

Maria lit a cigarette and exhaled.

"Get in line, buddy," she answered then walked out into the street and hailed a cab.

What's-his-name from Peixe was going to call when she got home to her apartment. She could sense it. It was just one of those nights.

CHAPTER FOUR

Anne was awoken by a knock at her door.

"Hello?" she called out.

Patricia entered the room. It was the first time in a week that Anne had seen her since coming to Talamh an Eisc.

"How have you been enjoying your R and R?" she asked.

Anne yawned and pulled the soft white cotton duvet around her. "I can't remember sleeping this well. I guess it helps that I'm not surrounded by people screaming at each other."

"The cork panelling in the walls really helps insulate sound," Patricia explained. "Discretion is a priority here."

"I see," Anne replied.

"Why don't you get dressed and meet me downstairs at the cabana by the pool for some breakfast."

Anne got ready and came down the grand staircase from the third floor to the grand hall. Talamh an Eisc's interior was dripping with silk, velvet, and gilded mouldings. Staff were cleaning sofas, chaises, and lush rugs with intricate stitching. Unlike clubs on Temple Street like Liban's, whose self-deprecating aesthetic was meant to fulfill voyeuristic Townie fantasies, Talamh an Eisc's artwork celebrated life in Kildare. Anne's favourite painting was of a fisherman hauling up a lobster pot. The fisherman's hands were at the heart of the canvas, the painter having lovingly detailed all the cracks and callouses in the old man's tight grip as he hauled a living from the sea.

Anne walked out onto the terrace and towards the pool. The water shone like a sapphire jewel, dappled by the sun's rays. A few girls were tanning in loungers beside the pool. In the cabana, Patricia was waiting a table with a plate of fried eggs, tomatoes, mushrooms, and toast dripping in butter. Beads of water dripped from a tall, skinny chilled glass of freshly squeezed orange juice. Anne sat down and took a drink. The sugars touched every nerve ending in her body. Patricia smiled and plunged the French press sitting in the middle of the table and poured them each a mugful, filling the air with a caramelized and nutty aroma.

"Aren't you having anything?" Anne asked, already halfway through her meal.

"I already ate," Patricia replied. She lit a cigarette and took a sip of coffee. "So, what do you think?"

Anne finished her breakfast with a mouthful of orange juice. "This is the most beautiful and extraordinary place I've ever been."

"But..." Patricia said, smiling.

"But," Anne repeated. "I'm a little weirded out by what goes on here. Certain places are out of bounds, particularly in the evening. I mean, I can guess what goes on here, but I don't understand where I fit in."

"I like to give the newcomers a week to enjoy themselves before we start assigning tasks. I want you to get a feel for the place before you engage with our clientele. A lot of rich and powerful men from Baccalieu come here. Like I said, discretion is a priority."

"What about phone calls? Whenever I ask someone about a phone they clam right up."

"Phone calls are a privilege here, which can take some getting used to. Again, discretion. We can't have people telling tales out of school."

"So, when do I get my phone call."

Patricia laughed. "You make it sound like you're in prison. I doubt the men at Cadeia are sitting poolside enjoying a meal like this." She snapped her fingers at the cabana's server and held up two fingers. "We'll get you working for awhile and see how you handle it."

"What will I be doing?"

"Just bartending to start. Tonight, you'll be working in the TK. We don't do Ink-ins here, but you do have a flare behind the bar. After that we'll see."

The server brought them two mojitos.

"We grow the citrus and mint here at our greenhouse," Patricia said.

Anne could taste the freshness. It was the best mojito she'd ever had.

"I can understand if you're a little uncomfortable with the way I run things here," Patricia continued. "But please trust me and give this place a chance. I really hope you can find a niche for yourself here. Once you get your bearings, we can talk about what you'd like to do."

"I have so many questions."

"Shoot."

"For starters, who even owns this place?"

"I do."

"How the hell did you find the money?"

"That's a very long story. Maybe another time. For now, let's just say that I'm good at recognizing talent and matching that with very specific demands. I'm a people person."

"Oh, come on. Don't be so prudish. This is like a casino, strip club, and brothel all rolled into one."

"I like to think of it as a gentleman's club."

"And you're the Madam Supreme."

"I guess you could call it that. My main preoccupation, aside from making sure everything runs smoothly, is extracting hidden desires from rich and powerful men. There's someone and something for everyone here. Role playing, submission, domination, femdom, the girlfriend experience. Both genders are available for hire. All fantasies are entertained. I make these men feel comfortable enough to share their fantasies then turn that information into an experience. Make it real."

"But how's that different from Temple Street?"

Patricia smiled. "See. You're just as smart as your brother. Unfortunately, as much as Merrow men are discriminated against, Merrow women are doubly so."

Anne waited for a response.

"The short answer is that we're building something here. Right under the noses of the Indesejável. Something that will turn everything upside down."

"And what's that?"

"You're just going to have to stick around and find out." Patricia rubbed out her cigarette into a crystal ashtray in the middle of the table. "Enjoy the rest of your day. Saturday night is our busiest night. You'll be tending bar in the conservatory."

Patricia got up and was about to leave.

"Tell me this at least," Anne said. Patricia waited. "What does 'Boudica' mean?"

"Why, it means me, of course."

Patricia left then, leaving Anne with only a confused look on her face.

"Anything else, miss?" the waiter asked her.

"Another coffee, please."

Anne lit herself a cigarette and took in the grounds. There was a large brick section at the back of the mansion. There were no windows or doors on the outside. As far as Anne knew, the only way in was a door on the third floor that was always locked. She wondered if it had something to do with what Patricia was building. The waiter brought her coffee. Its smell and flavour assuaged her curiosities for now.

* * *

The conservatory was a glorious array of dwarf fruit trees, rhododendrons, azaleas, pinks, purples, reds, greens, and blues. The fragrance alone made Anne happy to be working here. The fact that she didn't have to wear make-up and dress like a mermaid made it that much sweeter.

The work was easy. Businessmen, bankers, politicians, and gangsters collected their drinks then wandered around the conservatory, weaving around the marble statues, discussing deals comprised of ungodly sums of money. They tipped generously. However, Anne's heart broke whenever some drunken buffoon collapsed onto the flowers.

At the end of her shift, she sat down on a bench where a particularly fat Mafioso had fallen backwards and flattened a lovely batch of yellow roses. She picked up an undamaged bulb whose stem was cracked. The colour of its leaflets was so vibrant, like she held a tiny sun in her hands. Hopefully the thorns had ruined the man's expensive suit. She laid the flower on the bench then took the staff staircase at the back of the mansion up to third floor. A clock told her it was past 3 a.m.

When she got to the third floor, a line of hooded figures was making their way to the back of the mansion, to the door that was always locked.

"Hey," she said. "What are you guys doing?"

One of the figures removed their hood. It was the waiter who worked in the cabana.

"Boudica has not yet made you an initiate," he said. "Please, return to your room."

The rest of the group entered the room then shut the door, locking it. Anne shook her head and went to her room. She fell straight onto her bed, her feet thankful. The gentle tiredness spread up from her legs through her body, pushing away any confusion, replacing it with unencumbered sleep.

CHAPTER FIVE

In his fifteen years on the job, Kieran had seen more than his fair share of gruesome murders. A pregnant woman stabbed hundreds of times by an angry lover, charred bodies of arsonists, and the poor fuckers who dared testify against the gangs. Kieran used to think they were the worst. The gangs slashed up their faces and dumped their bodies in the Gut to bloat, all so their families couldn't hold open-casket funerals. But, as he ducked under the yellow tape and walked down the alleyway, he discovered that he'd never seen anything like this. The grim, bizarre, theatricality of it.

The body was painted all in black. Not just a really deep blue; pitch black. And there was a squid on top of his head. He was kneeling, as if in prayer, with his hands laid atop a bottle of Ink. A flashing light from the top of the building's side illuminated a small patch of the alley where the victim was found. It had clearly been placed here for someone to find it. Kieran crouched down for a closer look, covering his nose from the briny stench. He was used to spending time in rooms with so much blood it smelled like a bucket of rusty nails, but this body smelled like it had been dragged from the bottom of the ocean. It was difficult to tell with all the black paint, or whatever it was, but there didn't seem to be any sign of trauma. There was no sign of struggle around the scene, either. Not even a trail of black paint leading out of the alley. This was a busy part of downtown Kildare, close to the bars and the harbour. Bars emptied out between 3 a.m. and 4 a.m., then fishermen started arriving for work at around 5 a.m. That only left about an hour for all this to go down. Clearly, whoever did this was very familiar with the rhythms of the Gut.

"We got a call from a fisherman at around 4:45 a.m. saying there was a body here," the arriving officer explained. "The M.E. showed up soon after and confirmed he was dead."

Kieran stood up and went over to speak with the fisherman.

Patrolmen had the murder scene sectioned off, an alleyway just at the edge where Temple Street gave way to the fish market. A few people paused briefly then continued about their business; folks around here were used to homicide; the pause was only because there had been so few this summer—almost like seeing that old relative you'd forgotten about.

"I was on my way to the harbour," the fisherman explained. "I saw buddy down the alleyway. I figured he might have been some drunk or something, but it looked weird, so I checked him out, thought he might need help. Didn't take long for me to realize he was dead. That's when I went over to that payphone over there and called you guys."

"Did you see anyone else around here, leaving the scene?"

"No one. Listen, man, I got to get to work."

Kieran believed his story, but he was nevertheless reluctant to let him go because he knew that as soon as he reached the docks word would spread. Since there was no reason keep him there, he took his contact information and let him go. He estimated that he probably had about an hour with his scene before the media arrived and the circus started.

Dawn was breaking and the Gut was alive. The market was getting ready for the day's business and fishermen were in the process of heading out. They pulled their tiny punts and rodneys out into the bay from wooden wharves extending from the water's edge like arthritic fingers. Networks of rickety ladders clung to the rocky landwash, leading from the wharves to the fishermen's stages where they slaughtered and processed squid, octopus, lobster, crab, mussels, oysters, shrimp, pretty much anything that wasn't cod.

Santiago showed up with a cigarette in his mouth and a coffee in each hand. He handed one to Kieran.

"What do we got, Kier?" he asked.

"Hard to tell much of anything with the way he is," Kieran replied. "He has a youthful build, so I'm guessing he's probably in his twenties. I don't see any signs of trauma. He must've been killed somewhere else and moved here. We'll have to wait for the autopsy to tell us more."

"Why does he look like that?"

"I have some theories. Have a crack at it yourself first."

"Honestly? It looks like a sick joke to me."

"Why do you say that?"

"He's holding a bottle of Ink and is wearing a squid. That's obviously a reference to getting Inked. And he's painted black to look like Ink."

"I think you're spot on, detective."

"But why? What's the point?"

"I'm guessing it's an angry local. Trying to stir things up."

"But things have been so good."

"A lot of old wounds still left. Some people not ready to heal. I have a feeling we're going to see more of this."

Then the forensics team showed up to take pictures and search the scene more thoroughly for evidence, but Kieran suspected they wouldn't find anything. He directed the medical team to back the ambulance into the entry way of the alley to block any reporters coming around. Soon enough, they were at the tops of the buildings, looking down to take pictures and get a look at the scene. Once the forensics were finished their sweep, Kieran ordered the M.E. to load the body into the ambulance and bring it over to the morgue. With Santiago, he pushed through the crowd towards the car, repeating "no comment" to any reporters. They got in their car and turned on the siren, following the ambulance. Kieran knew that the only piece of evidence they had going for them was that body, and it probably wasn't going to tell them very much.

"I noticed his hair was black," Santiago said. "Do you think that was the paint?"

"If it wasn't then this'll be a fine end to our little summer of love."

CHAPTER SIX

Colleen handed Maria a cup of coffee—black as the devil but sweet as an angel, just the way Maria liked it—pushed a few strands of red wavy hair behind her ears and sat beside her on the couch.

"I know you're afraid," Maria said. "But things around here aren't going to change until good people like yourself are willing to come forward."

"I understand," Colleen said. "I always told myself that if I was ever in this position, I'd do the right thing. Easier said than done, I guess."

"If you agree to testify, I can get you some money from the department for an apartment in the city until this blows over."

"I'm not even scared for myself. It's my family."

"Is there anyone you know outside of Kildare that you can stay with?"

"I have a brother who teaches at the university. He has an apartment near campus. But he doesn't know about this and I don't want to involve him."

"That's fair."

Maria set her coffee down on the table and turned to face Colleen, whose once-beautiful face was bloated nearly beyond recognition. Gashes exposed pale flesh.

She cracked her swollen lips to speak but she could only croak, belching forth the yawning stench of brine. Strands wriggled in her throat, crawling upwards. A squid's tentacles emerged her mouth. That's when Maria woke up screaming. She kicked the blankets and fell onto the floor, crab-walking backwards away from the bed until she hit the wall. She sat there, hyperventilating in a cold sweat until a knock at her door brought her back to waking reality. This was her crappy apartment and she was by herself. Another sharp knock at her door and she got up to fetch her bathrobe. She opened the door and found her super with a concerned look on his face.

"Sorry," she said before he could speak. "I thought I saw a rat."

"Rat?" he exclaimed. "Don't tell me the rats are back."

"No, no, it was just a dream."

"Are you sure? I can bring you some traps."

"I'm covered. Sorry for the racket."

She closed the door and went back to bed, a mattress and box spring laid atop the floor. Beside her was a milk crate that served as a nightstand for a few bottles of whisky—some empty, some half-full. Without bothering to look, she shook a couple until she heard that heavy sloshing sound. At least what's-his-name was already gone and didn't witness that episode. She couldn't remember if it'd even been good. Well, if she wasn't drunk enough to keep from dreaming but still couldn't remember the sex then it couldn't possibly have been very good. She drank until her chest and throat burned and her nose forgot the smell of Colleen's corpse. It had been a while since she'd had the dream — or any dream for that matter. The clock hiding amidst the bottles told her that it was almost noon. She took another long mouthful from the bottle and cursed her own folly.

The bodega downstairs was serving grilled codfish sandwiches for lunch. Maria grabbed one and a cup of coffee then hailed a cab to take her to her office. She took the elevator up to her floor. When she opened her office door, she saw him sitting there, looking professorial in his tweed uniform. She should've realized the dream about Colleen was premonitory. Ms. Nunes gave her an apologetic smile.

"Dr. Gallagher," Maria said.

"Please," he said. "Call me Sean."

Maria ushered him into her office. Today just kept getting better.

She sat down to her desk. Sean Gallagher took the chair opposite. Despite their complicated history, Maria still thought she'd like to cut herself against those cheekbones. Above those high cliff lines sat two emerald green jewels cut likes almonds, which gave way to a milky white forehead kissed with freckles that was set afire by curly flames of blazing red hair. In the five years since she'd last seen him, he'd only grown more handsome, more distinguished. That was when she was still a cop. Dr. Sean Gallagher may have been a distinguished professor of history at the University of Baccalieu, but there was no mistaking he was from the Gut, no matter how much tweed he wore.

"You must think it's strange that I'm coming to you given our history," he said. "I'm sorry if I played any part in driving you from the force. That wasn't my intention when I wrote that op-ed in *The Baccalieu Times*."

"No, no," Maria said. "You helped me realize the BAPD wasn't the place for me. I should be thanking you."

"Still, I feel like a lot of the things I wrote were in anger. If I did it now, it'd be more objective."

"But not as impassioned, I'm sure. Everything you said was true and there's no need to feel bad about it."

"I want you to know that I don't hold you personally accountable at all."

"I understand that, and I thank you for saying it. Now, what I can do you for."

Sean seemed grateful for the opportunity to change gears. Maria could tell he was trying to ready himself for whatever preamble he'd prepared before going into this meeting.

"My sister, Anne, has gone missing," he said.

"Where and when was she last seen?" Maria asked.

"Over a month ago she left the bar where she works and hasn't been seen or heard from since."

Maria took a drag from her cigarette and gently blew the smoke from her nose. She could tell he didn't like it but didn't want to appear uppity.

"Plenty of girls leave the Gut..." she saw a flash of resentment flicker in his eyes when she said it,"...Kildare when they get enough money. They leave Baccalieu altogether. Go somewhere to get a clean slate. Escape. Maybe that's what your sister did."

"That's not like Anne," Sean answered. "She would've called. Or at least written me."

The metallic fan, the only relief in Maria's stuffy consulting office, clicked whenever it finished a cycle. The nights may have been cold in this early fall, but the days still carried that oppressive Baccalieu humidity. Maria could see dampness forming on Dr. Gallagher's creamy skin under those layers of tweed. Either he didn't mind or was determined not to show it.

"Tell me something," she said. "You're a university prof. right?" He nodded. "So, I'm assuming you live in one of the nice neighbourhoods near campus?" He nodded again. "Why didn't Anne come live with you?"

"She is stubbornly independent. I offered many times, but she didn't want to impose on me. Besides, there is still much discrimination in the city. An uneducated girl such as a herself could never find work there except as a maid, which she won't do. Besides, she's still keen on the...activities...that go on in Kildare."

After Sean's explanation, Maria waited. She wasn't sure what she was waiting for but something about his monologue didn't smell right. It felt too prepared, too rehearsed. He'd anticipated this question and built a defence around the real answer. Maria wanted the real answer and, in situations like these, silence was often the best offence.

"OK, I know," Sean said. "That's not a good enough explanation. I should've tried harder, reached out to her. If I'm being honest, there's always been a tension between us. Because I 'got out.' It's a tricky dynamic to navigate. Whenever I offer help, she interprets it as charity."

Maria sensed there was still more to this story but was content with this brief moment of self-flagellation.

"Have you gone to the police?" she asked.

"Oh sure, but they're not going to do anything. I don't have to tell you that. I spoke with Detective Hynes, your old partner. They've appointed him as the contact on these missing persons cases. It's nice the department thought to at least choose a Merrow for this, but it's just one man, so he's obviously overworked. He was the one who suggested I reach out to you."

Maria was silent.

"Kieran explained that you hadn't talked much since you left the force?"

"You said 'these missing persons cases.' There's a lot of that going on?"

"Oh yes. During this great 'Kildare Renaissance' as the politicians like to call it, instead of dead bodies, people are simply disappearing. As far as I can tell it's out of sight out of mind. I've tried to publish some op-eds about it in the papers, but no one wants to acknowledge it. They're too busy taking advantage of the economic opportunities this extended drop in crime has provided. I suspect this will all come crashing down if anyone dares to scratch the surface a little."

As he got more impassioned the facade withered and his adapted city speak gave way to Kildare brogue. The layers of sophistication were betrayed by a hard determination that could only come with growing up in a place like the Gut.

"So, will you take my case?" Sean asked.

Maria took a long final drag from her cigarette then rubbed it out in her ashtray. "I'm sorry, but, no, I can't."

"Detective Hynes said you'd be resistant, but that you were still the best chance I have."

"Detective Hynes should have told you that I haven't set foot in the G...Kildare in five years. I don't have the network or the sources anymore. I don't know that part of town like I used to. And frankly, I don't want to. Again, I'm sorry. I feel like I owe you a great debt, but I can't do this."

Sean's emerald eyes twinkled. Maria knew that look; she often had the same one when initially refused by a potential witness. This wasn't the end of it. That was alright; she was always a sucker for redheads. He stood up and shook her hand then left. Maria sat down and cursed her no-booze-in-the-office policy. She fetched herself another cigarette and smoked slowly. When it was finished, she got up to leave.

"He's as handsome as you said he was," Ms. Nunes said.

"I'm heading out for the day," Maria said. "Feel free to leave whenever."

She got in a cab and headed to the east side of town. Money in Baccalieu sprawled eastward and settled into multi-story houses of no particular architectural style aside from Big. Stone driveways led to monstrosities of dormers, pilasters, chimneys, and Palladian windows that overwhelmed the size of the owners' lots like tumours. She didn't miss the wide lawns and narrow minds. The cabbie pulled up outside her mother's house. She knocked on the door and Siobhan answered, her mother's Merfie housekeeper.

"Maria," she said. "I wish you had let us know you were coming."

"Why?" Maria asked. "Is this a bad time or something?"

Her mother came onto the landing with a glass in her hand and saw Maria standing in the foyer. She looked at the glass in her hand as if she were trying to come up with some explanation then decided she wouldn't bother. Her slippered feet descended the stairs slowly with uncertain steps. Maria now regretted her decision to come; she should've known that by the afternoon her mother would be good and sauced.

"And to what do I owe this pleasure of a visit from my daughter?"

"Just thought I'd drop by. It's been awhile."

"It certainly has."

Her mother sauntered into the living room. Maria followed.

The house was a sepulchre to her dead brother. Large marlin and swordfish that he'd caught adorned the walls. There were pictures of him along with his trophies and medals from swimming and rugby. Kieran was in one when they played together in boarding school. There were even a few pictures of her father. As far as Maria knew, her police certificate and newspaper clippings, along with her various other mementos, were packed away in boxes in her old room.

Her mother saw her looking at all the photos.

"It still feels like yesterday, doesn't it?" she said, her eyes getting glassy. "I should never have let him out on that boat that day. I gave him too much freedom, but boys need that."

Maria wasn't interested in rehashing her mother's merry-go-round of guilt and self-pity.

"How's your charity work going?" she asked.

"Excellent. The last gala was such a success. Why don't you come to our next meeting? I'm sure your experiences would give an interesting perspective."

Maria was initially touched by her mother's desire to include her. She usually treated her like radioactive waste, especially when it came to her social life. Perhaps she was trying to turn over a new leaf. But Maria didn't want to do the charity thing with all the other socialites. She didn't want to get dragged into that world. After all, it wasn't really about the charity, was it? It was more an excuse to drink and show off your money to all your other drunk, rich, sad, bored friends. Maria was, admittedly, all those things, but she preferred to stay home by herself.

"Not really my scene," she said.

"Oh sweetheart, why don't you just give up this private investigator racket? I know you joined the BAPD to prove a point, but look how that turned out. I can understand that you want to make a difference in the community. Surely, this would be better?"

Maria was silent.

"I realize now that after Luciano died, your father and I didn't give you the attention you needed. We should've been there for you. You tried to make the world a better place. That's very noble of you. But some people can't be helped. We do what we can, but there's a very good reason why so many Merfies end up in jail or worse. You shouldn't go on blaming yourself."

Maria stood up.

"Oh, honey, I'm sorry," her mother pleaded. "I didn't mean to offend you."

"It's fine," she said. "I have work to do. I'll see you later."

Her mother stood up carefully and walked towards her. They were never the hugging type, so Maria was unprepared for this. Ms. Costa paused before her daughter, unsure of what to do next. Maria took the initiative and gently wrapped her arms around her mother, feeling her tense body, clearly uncomfortable but insisting on all this nonetheless. They released each other and smiled. Maria walked towards the porch wondering if her mother was going senile.

"Anything else," Siobhan asked.

"Call me a cab?" Maria asked.

The maid nodded and left the foyer. Maria went out into the front terrace and smoked while she waited. That was enough penance for one day. Probably a month.

"Intersticio," she said to the cabbie when she got in.

Intersticio was on Eyre Square, the *de facto* red line between Kildare and Baccalieu. Some sentimentalist on the Baccalieu city council decided to erect a sculpture this summer, commemorating the first contact between the Indesejável and the Merrow. A cast zinc Merfie held a squid while a Townie held a cod. They were all smiles, except the fish. The council must've thought they ought to bestow a gift upon the Merfies for their recent good behaviour.

With all due respect to Peixe and Aloisio, Intersticio was the best club in the city. They served Merfie dishes of molluscs and crustaceans with spicy Townie flavours. Much like the food, the house band, The Celtiberians, played free form jazz that combined the melodic variation of Kildare and the clave patterns in Townie rhythms. The owners claimed it was the oldest tavern in the whole city. It started ages ago when Indesejável first began settling permanently. Before they could really understand each other (and before the Indesejável forced the Merrow to learn their language) they let their music do the talking.

Maria sat at the bar, sipping a gin and tonic. She watched The Celtiberians through the thick gauze of smoke that filled Intersticio. They were playing a bluesy jam. A few suitors dropped in to offer her a drink, but she wasn't interested tonight. She'd long mastered the ability to look into a man's eyes and tell him "no" with the exact amount of firmness that discouraged any further attempts without garnering the "bitch!" outbursts; although after a few drinks the latter became much more probable.

A large body entered her peripheral vision and sat down beside her. Without bothering to look, she could identify him from the easy grace with which he carried such mass.

"Pint of stout and big bowl of your spicy mussels," Kieran said.

The bartender served Kieran his drink.

"You know," he said to no one in particular. "One of these days some unscrupulous Townie is going to realize there's a fortune to be made mass marketing Merfie food, and we won't even see a dime."

Kieran paused when he said 'unscrupulous.' He always took pride in his education. He liked to carefully select and savour a word the way a glutinous child selects the most choice cookie in the jar. Maria didn't say a word and just kept listening to the music.

"This stuff isn't really my sorta thing," he continued,

gesturing towards the band with his pint of stout. "But it's hard not to appreciate talented musicians."

Maria took a drag and ignored him.

"I mean, why don't they play something with a little more swing? Something with a beat you can dance to. Everyone can enjoy that. The blues is fine when you're nursing a beer by the radio, crying over your old lady. When I go out, I want to have some fun."

She knew that was bait, but she might as well start talking unless she wanted to endure Kieran's opinions on music.

"You have until I'm finished this drink," she said.

"Sean Gallagher. He tells me you didn't accept his case. Why not?"

"You know why not."

"It's been five years."

"I still dream about her."

The bass player took over from the pianist with long sorrowful legatos.

"If you're so spooked by Kildare then why are you here, right on the border?" Kieran asked. "You're trying to face it. You just need a little push."

"Is that what this is about? You're trying to play armchair psychologist with me?"

"No. OK, fine, maybe a little. I can't help acting like a big brother sometimes. Mostly, I need your help. People are going missing in the Gut. Gangsters and working girls. It doesn't seem like it, but I can't help but think they're connected somehow. Then today, I got one of the weirdest cases I've ever seen in my career."

He looked around to make sure no one was eavesdropping. Maria was paying attention now; Kieran wasn't one for hyperbole.

"It was like some kind of ritual sacrifice. Like something you'd read about in an anthropology book. Guy was painted black and positioned like he was praying with a bottle of Ink in his hands. Just about no forensic evidence. Had to have been done somewhere else and brought there. Staged in an alleyway like it was meant to be discovered. Sound weird to you?"

Maria drank and remained silent.

"I think it all has something to with this 'Kildare Renaissance.' The media and the politicians all want to act like everything is best kind and hold hands, but there's something rotten going on. My only leads are female witnesses, and they won't open up to me. There's no female detectives on the force and the department won't give me any more resources."

Maria laughed. "You think they're going to give a shit. It's the wrong kind of people missing."

She took one last drag from her cigarette and rubbed it out in the ashtray. It was Kieran's turn to be quiet now.

"You still have faith in the badge after all this time," she said. "You know what I realized when I quit the BAPD? We can't stop it. There's no amount of detectives, cops, lawyers, district attorneys, arrests, sentences, plea bargains, or jail cells that can stop this. And you're definitely not going to stop it when the ones making all the decisions can't even see the Gut from their office windows. All this shit goes a long way back, but the system is still run by the kind of people that started it in the first place. They can double the amount of Merrow like yourself on the force and it still won't make a difference."

"So, we should give up?" Kieran asked. "Progress takes time."

"What you're talking about is glacial."

"Y'know, as a Merfie who came up through the BAPD, you'd think I'd have a little more empathy for women trying to break through, but I was just like other guys. Didn't think women had it in them. Weren't made for the job. All that bullshit. Then, when you were assigned to me as my partner, I didn't expect much, but you showed me wrong."

"What's your point?"

"Change is possible. And sometimes it happens in unexpected ways. You got to keep at it."

Maria took a drink.

"I know you haven't given up," Kieran continued. "You act like you do this PI gig for booze money, but we both know that's bullshit."

"Is it?" she asked.

"C'mon. How much is that harbour front property worth? Must be a small fortune."

"I sold it."

"Yeah right. Your poker face is still strong, I'll give you that, but there's no way you sold off your father's investments. Maybe you give the money away, maybe you give it to your mother. Maybe you rent at cost. That, I don't know. What I do know is that you don't have to be doing what you're doing. And even if that were true, most PIs don't take the sort of cases you do. Oh sure, your main clientele are rich gold diggers, but I know that you help out a lot of less wealthy women stuck in bad marriages or small-time entrepreneurs trying to navigate the Baccalieu mob."

"There you go with your armchair psychology." She finished her drink and waved at the bartender for another. "All done."

"Alright, I'll stop." Kieran pulled out a picture from his pocket and slid it across the bar to Maria. "She needs you. No one else is going to give a shit."

Maria couldn't help but steal a quick glance at Anne's photo. Kieran finished his drink and stood up.

"You should stick around," she said. "They usually do jiggs and reels after the blues. Real lively. Right in your wheelhouse."

He left the photo there and walked away.

Fuck him and fuck Kildare. Fuck Baccalieu and the BAPD. Fuck this whole goddamn city. She was going to be damn well sure tonight to drink enough to forget the whole lot of it. And, hopefully, get laid while she was at it.

A tall, lanky Townie from across the bar locked eyes with her. She didn't really like the skinny ones, but the ring on his finger meant no commitments and likely an early morning getaway. The photo of Anne stared at her from the counter in accusation. She shoved it in her pocket quickly before buddy made his way over.

* * *

She woke up in her bed at 5 a.m. Her blankets were soaking wet and the room stunk like brine. There was a body lying next to her. What's-his-name was still here.

"Hey," she said. "Did you piss the fucking bed?"

She shook him. The body was cold, bloated, and stiff with rigor mortis. Maria threw the blankets off and found Colleen's corpse lying next to her. She covered her mouth to keep from screaming and shut her eyes. Hot tears forced their way out of her eyelids. She slapped herself in the face until it stung. When she opened her eyes, Colleen was gone, and the bed was dry. No more smell of brine.

There was no sense trying to go back to sleep, so she went over to the window and had a smoke. The city was coming alive under the dawn-blue sky. After her second cigarette, she grabbed the phone.

"Hello?" Sean Gallagher's tired voice asked.

"I'll take your case," she said then hung up before he could say thanks.

CHAPTER SEVEN

Kieran let out a long exhalation when Dr. Chavas pulled back the sheet and revealed the pale youthful face of Gaspar Reis. The stink of brine cut through the disinfectant that permeated the morgue.

"Sorry for the delay," Dr. Chavas explained. "It took us a long time to remove the ink from his face without damaging the skin. We still haven't been able to identify what it is exactly."

"Let's head over to the Reis family right away," Kieran said to his partner.

They left the morgue and drove towards the east end of the city.

"This is worse than I expected," he said.

"Why?" Martim asked. "Who is this kid?"

"His name is Gaspar Reis. He's just some punk kid from the east end. Sometimes got in trouble for hanging out with low-level Mafiosos, selling designer drugs to kids, that kind of stuff."

"So he's a rich kid?"

"Very rich. He's parents have all kinds of connections. Gaspar liked to hang around in Kildare to pick up drugs at the harbour or have some fun on Temple Street. Wannabe-gangster stuff. But every so often he'd show up on our radar and we'd have to handle it delicately."

"Sounds like they're gonna make some noise."

"You bet. I can already see how it's going to play out in the media world. Naive and innocent Baccalieu boy seduced and killed by Kildare's temptations."

"Do you think this has anything with all those disappearances you've been tracking?"

"I don't know. My guess is that Gaspar got desperate and started selling in Kildare. Maybe whoever is behind all this wanted to send a message. But that doesn't really fit the mould, does it? Why would they suddenly change up, especially with a Townie kid?"

"Unless that's the point," Martim said.

Kieran considered this for a while before they pulled up outside the Reis family mansion.

"You should take lead here," he said.

Martim nodded.

* * *

They stood in the Reis family's living room. Matilde Reis cried into the arms of her husband, Celso. Kieran was as used to this as someone could become. Martim was stiff and unsure what to do. The couple hadn't offered the detectives a seat, so they remained standing.

The time between the parents' sobs swelled. When it was clear that they'd crested that first wave of grief, Kieran exhaled and rocked back on the balls of his feet to signal Martim it was time to start.

"Mr. and Mrs. Reis," Martim started. "If you could tell us anything about the sort of people Gaspar was involved with, it might lead us to his killer."

"I'll tell you right now who killed my son," Mr. Reis said. "Those goddamn Merfies in the Gut."

The detectives were silent. Mr. Reis was momentarily embarrassed when he remembered Kieran was in the room. Then, instead of apologizing, he jutted his chin in silent defiance.

"Gaspar was a sweet boy," Mrs. Reis insisted. "But he got involved with drugs and it got worse from there."

The Reises began a heavily redacted account of their wayward son's life, their attention focused exclusively on Martim. The detectives took perfunctory notes to appear respectfully attentive to this rough draft of their son's eulogy.

"If you think of anything else that could be relevant to this case, please don't hesitate to call," Martim handed them his card. "Sorry for your loss."

The detectives left the Reis' home and got into their cruiser.

"Fuck me, doesn't that just piss you right off?" Martim asked Kieran. "I mean, it's so obvious this little shit was a spoiled brat and they don't want to take any responsibility. And the way they gawked at you, man, it's like they blamed you."

"I'm starting to think he was targeted," Kieran said.

"How so?"

"Like he was specifically chosen to cause as big a splash as possible. Gaspar's body was dramatically staged. On top of that, he comes from a rich east end family. Whoever did this wanted a lot of attention."

"What about the League of Indesejável Supremacy? You think they'd plant a false flag? Maybe they're trying to disrupt all this goodwill that's been building between Kildare and Baccalieu."

"I don't think so. Spilling Indesejável blood seems too blasphemous a means for them no matter what the end. Still, it's worth chasing down."

"What if there's a mirror group in Kildare that we haven't heard about yet? Like a Merfie...I mean...Merrow supremacist organization?"

"That's also a possibility. First, I want to hit up Ballybane Road for any potential witnesses. Just to cross it off the list."

"If you say so."

They drove into Kildare, to the stretch of row houses a few blocks up from the harbour. Despite driving in an unmarked car, the locals instantly began announcing the arrival of the 'peelers.' All activity and transactions ceased, and everyone assumed their best behaviour.

"Wait here," Kieran said.

Martim watched as his partner left the safety of the car and strolled up to a couple of dealers without so much as a hint of hesitation in his stride. Kieran chatted with the gang bangers for a few minutes then headed back towards the car.

"They said they'd seen someone fitting Reis' description trying to sell drugs here recently," he said when he was back inside. He turned the car on and left Kildare.

"Do you think they killed him?" Martim asked.

"No, I don't. Look around you. Business here has been booming since the BAPD started its 'laissez-faire' approach. They don't need to worry about competition. Turf doesn't mean what it used to."

"What do you wanna do now?"

"Let's split up. There's no point in me going to the League's lodge, so you tackle that on your own. I'll see if I can find some leads on a Merrow angle."

Kieran drove towards the station.

"So you don't agree with the laissez-faire model?" Martim asked.

"I didn't say that. It's certainly given us the opportunity to follow up more on the domestic cases. But, as you can see, the drug problem is worse than ever. We just don't see it because it's gone indoors."

"The homicides have dropped way off."

"True."

"But you don't think that's because of police policy?"

Kieran hesitated.

"You can trust me," Martim said. "I'm not going to tattle."

"No, I don't think it's because of police policy. Or at least, that's only part of the story. I think it's got something to do with all the missing persons."

"How so?"

"Someone managed to get a stranglehold of the black market in Kildare without leaving a trail of blood. I don't know who or how, but they managed to knock off the big players. Of course, people are all too happy for them to be gone without asking inconvenient questions."

"And do you think that all has something to do with Gaspar Reis?"

"Maybe."

They pulled into the station and Kieran got out. Martim took the cruiser to go question the League. Kieran went inside and called his wife from his desk phone.

"Hi, darling," he said. "How's it going?"

"Good. Just finishing getting supper ready. You running late?"

"A little bit. Shouldn't be any more than an hour. Definitely enough time to get back and put Aoife to bed."

"Good luck."

"Love you."

"I love you, too."

* * *

Martim thought that he'd done a good job concealing his anxiety when Kieran asked him to hit up the Knights' Lodge on his own. Knowing Kier, it was likely a test. Other guys on the force tried to dismiss that as Kier flexing on his terf, but now, parked outside the Lodge, Martim understood that it took guts. He took one last second to look in the mirror and get into character.

A tall, serious-looking man stood casually by the door, smoking a cigarette. As Martim approached, the serious-looking man didn't move and kept his eyes on the street. Martim opened his jacket to display his badge. The serious-looking man stepped aside and opened the door, still keeping his attention on the street.

The Lodge was mostly empty. A few guys shot pool. They all had shaved heads and wore golf shirts with suspenders and Doc Martens. The game stopped as Martim entered. Everyone turned to watch him, silent. Martim walked towards the bar, not allowing his attention to linger anywhere.

The bartender approached but didn't speak.

"Ginger and rye," Martim said.

The bartender remained indifferent to his request. Martim could feel the pool players take a few steps closer to the bar. He opened the flap of his jacket to show his badge. The bartender turned around and started preparing a ginger and rye. The pool game resumed as well as the banter. But Martim knew they were all keeping an ear out for him.

"I'm looking for Freddy," he said. Might as well get straight to the point.

"He's not here," the bartender said with his back to Martim, cleaning a glass.

"Yeah, well, I got something he might want to hear. Police business."

The bartender disappeared into a swinging door behind the bar. He soon emerged with Frederico Da Rocha following behind. Nearly sixty now, Freddy was still a physical presence. He sat beside Martim and considered him with his intense blue eyes set deep beneath a low forehead.

"What brings you all the way here from the Gut, Detective Santiago," Freddy said. "Don't be surprised. I take an interest in all the promising young officers making their way up the ladder at the BAPD. As you know, I have a lot of friends there."

Martim finished his ginger and rye and set it down. A smile broke across Freddy's big mouth and imposing jaw.

"Another for my friend here, Hugo," Freddy said. "And one for me, too."

The bartender got them their drinks.

"Hugo says you have something to say that might interest me. Let's hear it."

"That murder on Temple Street was a Townie kid by the name of Gaspar Reis."

"I'm sorry to hear that. What's it got to do with me."

"You want to tell me where you were that night."

Freddy laughed. Hugo joined in and so did the guys playing pool.

"You think I had something to do with that?"

Martim remained silent.

"Fine. Just so no one can say Frederico Da Rocha doesn't comply with the police, I was home with my wife and kids. You can call the missus right now. She'll tell you."

"I'll give her a call later."

"You guys must really be out on a limb if you're coming here to brace me."

"You've been very vocal lately about the improving relations between Baccalieu and Kildare."

"I'm a concerned citizen who doesn't want to see crime spreading from the Gut into our fine neighbourhoods."

"You're not going to tell me the Knights suddenly believe the pen is mightier than the sword."

"Oh, we have a reputation, I can't deny it. Dealing with those savages, we've sometimes had to protect ourselves. But, Detective, I'm frankly insulted that you think we'd kill one of our own to achieve our goals. Indesejável blood is precious."

"So you've never targeted inter-racial couples?"

Freddy smiled; his blue eyes beamed.

"Take your time, Detective. Ask any of my boys where

they were that night and feel free to follow up on their alibis." He stood up. "The detective's drinks are on the house, Hugo." He patted Martim on the shoulder. "I won't take this little powwow personally. I understand you have to follow every lead and I respect that you came to me straight." He rubbed out his cigar in the ashtray. "Take care now."

Interviewing the other members was an exercise in futility. They'd clearly been coached to clam up when talking to police. The alibi everyone offered was that they were here at the Lodge. Even when Martim tried to misdirect them, they'd double down. Q: Can you tell me where Agastinho was the night of the murder? A: Here with me at the Lodge. Q: He told me he was with his girlfriend? A: No, he's mistaken, he was here. Kieran might have been able to lure them into a trap, but Martim hadn't yet mastered those chess moves. He got everyone's statement for the sake of procedure and left. Driving, he lowered his window and felt the breeze. The air was sticky with humidity until he got enough speed. The breeze cooled his face and he felt his chest start to loosen. He was going to need some more ginger and rye when he got home.

* * *

Kieran drove over to Baccalieu University. There was a sense of timelessness on the campus amidst the classical rotundas, stone fountains, and ivy-covered brick walls populated by young students dressed in modern styles. Kieran was pleased to see a few redheads peppered amidst the Townies. A small step forward from when he and Sean were the only Merrow on campus.

He made his way to the library and walked down the staircase to the basement where the old archives were. There he found Sean's office. He knocked and entered.

"They really got you locked away down here in the dungeon," Kieran said.

Sean looked up from an old manuscript he was reading.

"I may not see natural light for hours at a time, but I have the largest office on campus," he replied.

"What are you working on?"

"This is an old balance sheet from a merchant's accountant. Just trying to collate some data."

"Sounds exciting."

"Not the sexiest part of the job, but it's important to back up some of my arguments. By the way, Ms. Costa has agreed to take on my case. Thank you."

"Save the gratitude for her when she gets the job done, which I'm sure she will."

"So, detective, what brings you to my dungeon?"

"How much have you heard about the recent body that was found near Temple Street?"

"Just what the papers have published."

"I'm about to let you in on some confidential information. I trust you'll keep it to yourself."

"Of course."

Kieran's shoulders finally relaxed for the first time today. He didn't like to admit it, but he always noticed it happen whenever he was solely in the presence of Merrow. Being around Townies all day meant wearing a mask that he often forgot he wore. Its edges dug into his skin and it was always a relief to take it off.

"The victim was a young Indesejável male, known to authorities as a low-level drug dealer," Kieran explained. "He was found coated in some kind of black tar. He was kneeling, as if in prayer, holding a bottle of Ink and a squid atop his head."

"I see. Clearly, some sort of reference to the 'Getting Ink'd' ritual."

"I remember you writing an op-ed criticizing the practice."

"Are you saying I'm a suspect?"

"No," Kieran laughed. "You're not the only Merrow who doesn't like it. I'm hoping you could help me understand what it might have to do with a homicide."

"I can't presume the killer's motives, but I can tell you my issue with it. Not only is it a fake tradition, it serves to gloss over the complex history of our interactions with the colonizers. It perpetuates the narrative that relations were peaceful and amicable. And as time went on, we simply couldn't get on board with the colonizers' 'advanced' society, which is why we have so much lawlessness in Kildare."

"So, whoever we're after is some kind of history buff."

"Possibly. More importantly, I would say that they are focused on disrupting relations between Indesejável and Merrow."

"This seems like pretty obscure stuff. Not exactly mainstream."

"The real history about how the dynamic between us and the colonizers evolved is controversial. Hence my digging through these papers to cover all my bases."

"They weren't teaching that stuff when I was a student here so you're going to have to fill me in."

"When the colonizers first arrived, we showed them the ropes of the inshore cod fishery. We also taught them how to fish for bottom feeders like lobster, crab, and shrimp. Some of the colonizers started staying year-round, and eventually began adopting our beliefs and rituals. The 'Ink'd' trend is a sanitized version of this history."

"They shared our beliefs? You weren't kidding about the 'controversial' thing."

"I only have a job here because the university wants to show they're not discriminating. My efforts to establish a Department of Merrow Studies nearly died on the vine because of interdepartmental hostility and indifference. Luckily, my work is highly esteemed by other universities on the continent."

"So what happened? What changed between us and them?"

"There was a great storm followed by a giant wave that nearly wiped out the city. A real tsunami. Nothing like it before or since. A lot of people died; a lot of merchants lost money. For whatever reason, they blamed us. From then on, it was illegal for us to practice our traditions and certainly illegal for any Indesejável to partake in them. That was also when we were banned from fishing cod and only allowed the bottom feeders. And, of course, prostitution. From this point on you start to see the proliferation of stigmatizing merfolk. 'Fishing and fucking.' That sort of thing."

"They blamed us for a storm?"

"It goes deeper than that, I think. Reading over these

old manuscripts and correspondences I can't help but feel there's this great unspoken thing, a taboo. There's mention of 'sealing the caves' along with 'ending the traditions.' Also, even rarer, is talk of concealing some book so that it might not get into the wrong hands. I think there were some kind of strange rituals going on between our ancestors and the colonizers in a cave somewhere, which they attribute to causing this storm."

"And that's what you're trying to prove."

"Yes, exactly."

"It would help if you could find that book they were talking about."

"That's what I find most interesting. There's never mention of destroying it, only hiding or concealing it."

"I guess there was something inside it they didn't want destroyed."

"Yes, that's one explanation."

"What's the other?"

Sean smiled. "Perhaps it can't be destroyed," he said.

"What do you mean, 'can't?'"

"I'm sorry, it's just conjecture at this point until I can find some real evidence. Despite my stodgy professorial demeanour, I'm a romantic at heart."

Kieran stood up.

"Thank you for your time, Professor."

"Any time."

As he was heading out, Kieran noticed a small wooden sculpture on one of Sean's bookcases. It was a tiny merfolk, with a fish's tail, a skeletal body, and the head of a devil. It was presenting its fangs and claws like it was swimming to attack.

"Nasty little guy," Kieran remarked.

"Much of my research is about the way Merrow have commodified the Indesejável's perception of us."

"They want to see us as devils, so we might as well make a buck off it."

"Exactly."

"I guess that's your whole issue with the 'Getting Ink'd' stuff."

"I suppose so."

"What other options do we have?"

"Unfortunately, there are no easy answers. Don't get me wrong. I don't blame any Merrow trying to make some money. I actually find it quite ingenious. But if we're going to advance our case for equality, we're going to have to become more critical of these sorts of things."

"You've certainly contributed more than your fair share in that regard."

Kieran turned to shake Sean's hand when he noticed how exhausted the professor's eyes looked. A specific type of exhaustion that came from too much sorrow. He'd seen the same look in Maria's eyes when she quit the force. He felt compelled to reach out and hug Dr. Gallagher. Tell him everything was going to be OK, that they were going to find his sister, and all this bullshit—the discrimination, the double standards, the bigotry—would be over soon.

Instead, he turned around and left.

CHAPTER EIGHT

Maria had spent an hour wandering up and down Ballybane Road, struggling to reacquaint herself. The game had changed, and she didn't understand these new rules. Touters announced their product and customers entered and exited the row houses like some kind of farmer's market. No one solicited Maria. Trade seemed strong enough that the hard sell wasn't necessary. They probably figured she was a cop or a journalist or just another Townie tourist coming to gawk at the junkies. She was about to flash some money to try to make a connection when she heard a familiar, crackly voice.

"Maria?"

She turned and saw Fin O'Rourke approaching her.

"It's good to see you, Fin." And she meant it. Aside from finding someone who could guide her through this new landscape, she was happy to see that Fin had managed to survive another five years on the streets. But that didn't surprise her. Anyone who could survive a heroin addiction into their forties had a mind that saw angles in a circle. Maria could see now, though, that the years were finally starting to catch up with him. Her eyes moved from his hand leaning hard against the aluminum hospital cane to his battered forearms, swollen and pocked like tattered leather. The intelligence behind his eyes that once burned clear and bright had faded to a dull glimmer. It was still there, nevertheless, not yet wholly swallowed up by his addiction.

"You know, I should be giving you a hard time," he said. "It's been five years, girl. You don't call, you don't write. I heard you left the force but damn, you can at least come see your old friend."

"You're right, Fin. I apologize."

"So what brings you back to the neighbourhood?"

"I'm here for a client. His sister is missing. Have you heard much about these disappearances?"

Fin looked around nervously and shifted on his swollen ankles. "Ah, well, y'know, I dunno much about any of that."

Maria rolled her eyes and produced a few bills from her wallet. Fin refused.

"No, no, it's not like that," he said.

"Well, what's it like? Tell me. How about I buy you lunch. Squid rings at McDonagh's."

Fin hesitated. His anxiety battled with his hunger and conscience.

"Alright," he said. "Give me an hour."

"You on shift or something?"

"Yeah, I announce the product. How much and where. Direct people and such."

"So, instead of the old touter, you're now like a maitre d' for users."

"Exactly. People recognize my word means a lot in these parts, see."

"Alright, well, when your break is up, I'll be waiting

for you. Meet me at the park bench near the harbour, our usual spot."

Maria watched Fin return to his post, and she felt herself sink back into the rhythms of the Gut. Whatever new equilibrium Kildare had reached with regards to homicide wasn't going to stop the rot at its centre. Ballybane and all the other drug corners and brothels in the Gut were rooted in desire. People wanted pleasure, be it sex or drugs, and when there was a demand there would eventually be supply. More than that, Ballybane gave people like Fin a place where they could belong. Not everyone could fish, and there were very few opportunities for even exceptional people like Sean Gallagher, so the rest had to go somewhere. Ballybane welcomed them all. The users and the dealers, the prostitutes and pimps, the snitches and the stick-up crews all found a niche in this ecosystem. Even the BAPD found shape and meaning from Ballybane. That's why it couldn't be stopped, because if they really wanted to, they'd have to tear everything down to the studs and re-start. Face the realization that all the laws and institutions that Baccalieu were based upon were flawed. But the powers that be weren't ready for such an existential reckoning.

Maria made her way to McDonagh's. The place was packed as usual. Conversations halted when she entered; McDonagh's was far afield for a Townie. She ordered a basket of squid rings then found a table. There were murmurs of "five-oh" and "fella killed...painted black." It felt like she was a plainclothes detective all over again. The key was a quiet confidence, owning your space but not like you own the place. Too much timidity and they'll chew you up and spit you out. Too much arrogance and the Merfies would take offence. But despite whatever hostility she felt, she knew she wouldn't be denied service. This was a one-way street in Baccalieu. Townies could come and spend money in the Gut, but aside from a few maids and cabbies, Merfies couldn't bring their business across the red line.

"Costa!" the server called out.

She was startled when she heard her name. Happy to not have to spend another moment packed like a sardine in a can, she grabbed her calamari and left, making her way towards the harbour. She sat down on the old bench where she used to meet Fin when she was a cop. She picked at a few rings and watched the ink-covered fishermen working in the Gut, hoisting their nets of squid.

She heard feet shuffling and looked over to see Fin hobbling towards her with his cane. He sat down, looked around for any potential interlopers, then reached out for the rings and devoured them in about five minutes. She noticed that the grease-stained newspaper wrapped around the rings had a story about the Temple Street homicide that Kieran mentioned.

"Hungry?" she asked.

"Sorry," he laughed. "Haven't had a feed of this in ages."

"So, about those disappearances," she said.

Fin stopped licking his fingers.

"To be honest, I don't know much about them. What I can tell you is that any of the boys start acting up, no one sees or hears tell of them again. Anyone who talks too much tends to get disappeared, too."

"So a gang is taking out rivals. Big deal."

"No, it's not like that. They dis-ah-pear." Fin emphasized each syllable. "No sound of guns or a fight. They just vanish into the air."

"Is it the mafia?"

"The mafia is just about gone from Ballybane. Whoever is supplying, it's not them. And anyone who is caught selling Townie product is disappeared. But it looks like the mafia are trying to squeeze in again now. Probably think the place is for the taking now that bodies aren't being stacked up, I guess."

"And this new open-air drug market? Who's in charge?"

"Dunno. Man tells me every morning what the product is and where to direct customers."

"The cops just let it go on?"

"Yeah, so long as everyone plays nice."

Maria wasn't surprised. Most people didn't care about Merfies getting high so long as they weren't violent. But, she wondered, how long until bourgeois Townies get anxious once Merfies are no longer filling up the prisons and, god forbid, start accumulating wealth?

"What about girls?" she asked. "I've heard that good looking, young working girls are going missing, too."

"Well, a man like myself doesn't have the means to avail myself of that sort of company, if you know what I mean."

"The girl I'm looking for used to work at a strip club. Liban's."

"Your best bet would be to hit up a brothel on Jellybean Row. They'd probably know more. Now, if you're willing to foot that bill as well, I could be of some assistance."

Maria rolled her eyes.

"So? What's up?" Fin asked. "Tell me about this case that so suddenly brought your back to the Gut."

"This is a PI case I took on. Hynes reached out to me because he thinks the missing gangsters and working girls are related somehow."

"No, I mean what's up with you? How you doing? There's all kinds of sorrow and trouble behind those eyes. Don't think I can't see it."

Maria stood up and handed Fin a fiver. This time he took it.

"If there's really a Boogieman snatching people up in the Gut, maybe you should lay low for a day or two after talking to an outsider, especially a former murder cop. It was nice seeing you, Fin."

"Yeah, Detective, you too."

* * *

Maria made her way over to the red-light district of Kildare, the colourful stretch of row houses known as Jellybean Row. A motley of lavender, mauve, amber, magenta, jade, and flamingo clapboards were designed to attract foreign sailors from the harbour. And it looked like they'd gotten a fresh coat of paint since Maria was last here. The stoops were well maintained and there were even some plants and shrubs. Clearly, there was some money being put into the place. She picked the yellow house.

A plush velvet rug was spread out on the hardwood floor. Every archway was concealed by thick plumb curtains. An old man sat on a chaise longue, not making eye contact. To the right of the door she entered was another man standing behind a greeter's podium with a full-toothed grin.

"Officer Costa," the man announced. "Or is it still 'Officer?' Haven't seen you around these parts much these days. Heard you quit."

Maria recognized bow-legged Billy Yetman, or 'Yeti' as he was known back when she was a cop. A low-level pimp, it seemed that he'd transitioned to low-level bordello bouncer as prostitution had moved almost exclusively indoors in the Gut.

"Where's the madam?" Maria asked.

"You looking for work?" he asked. "My, my, how the mighty really have fallen."

Maria grabbed Yeti's balls in a vice-grip, hard enough for him the feel the sharpness of her nails through his slacks. He inhaled and froze still.

"Please excuse our man's manners," an older woman said as she entered the room. "Or lack thereof. How can I help you?"

"Looking for someone who can show a girl a good time," Maria said then released Yeti from her grasp. He stepped away and tried to regain some sense of his previous swagger.

"I'm sorry," the madam said. "We don't employ men here."

"If I wanted a man to disappoint me, I'd go to Temple Street and drag off whatever shrimp dick I wanted."

"I understand. Please, follow me. I think I know a few girls who would be suitable for you."

Maria stared down Yetman as she followed the madam, daring him to grin.

When the madam brought Maria into the parlour to show her a line-up of girls, it didn't take her long to choose. They posed seductively in their corsets, slips, and nightgowns. One girl stood out immediately. Her make-up wasn't quite refined, and she didn't seem so comfortable in her satin negligee. The shyness was real, not coy. She hadn't yet mastered the illusion. Maria walked up to her and took her hand.

"A fine choice," the madam said.

The girl led Maria to her room. The walls were covered with floral paper. Lace curtains covered the windows and the bed was surrounded by a sheer canopy. Maria thought it was pretty classy, aside from the mirror above the bed.

"My name's Aileen," the girl said.

"Maria."

"It's been awhile since I was with a lady," Aileen said, leaning towards Maria's lips.

"It's not like that," Maria said, holding the girl's hands before she could slip off her negligee. "I'm looking for information. I'm a private investigator. Sit."

"I don't want any trouble."

"Don't worry, you're not in any. It's about the working girls going missing here. I'm trying to track one of them down. She was a dancer. Anne Gallagher. Ring a bell?"

"I don't know anything about that."

"Come on, Aileen. I'm sure you've heard stories. Anything at all can help me. I'm sure you've had friends go missing, too."

Aileen bit her lip and considered it. "I can tell you what

I know, but the madam is gonna know that we didn't do nothing. She can tell."

Maria pulled off her belt, folded it between her two hands and snapped it. "Come on," she said. "Play along."

Aileen let out a little squeal. Maria was impressed. The girl had skill.

"OK," Maria said. "Start talking."

"I hear there's a madam that goes around looking for the best girls to come work at her brothel. It's supposed to be real chichi. A big mansion where the girls go live. Whenever any of them go, we never hear from them again. But it's supposed to be real nice. And we're not supposed to talk about it."

Snap. Squeal.

"Have you met this woman?"

"Once. When I first started, she came and had a look at me. She said I wasn't ready yet, but I had potential."

Snap. Squeal.

"What do you mean? How does she pick the girls?"

"She just looks at you. She's got these crazy intense eyes that look right through you. Felt like she was looking right into my soul, y'know? You kinda remind me of her to be honest."

"She's a Townie?"

"No, she's a Merfie. But I mean, like, the way she looks at people."

Snap. Squeal.

"Do you know where her brothel is? This mansion?"

"Not sure. I hear it's up in the hills somewhere."

"The hills? That's where rich Townies build their gated communities."

"That's all I know."

Snap. Squeal.

"The girls go willingly? Even though no one hears from them again?"

"It's a chance, y'know, to get out of the gutter. To something better."

"Does this madam drive a special car?"

"Yeah, it's a big fancy black coupe. With a mermaid statue on the hood."

Maria put her belt back on.

"Thanks," she said and gave Aileen a tip. "You've been a big help."

"You know, you can get into a lot of trouble asking around about this sort of stuff."

"I'm used to it."

"Do you think it's real?"

"What? The mansion?"

"Yeah."

"I guess that's what I have to find out."

Aileen started to cry. "I'd do anything to get out of here," she said.

Maria handed the girl her card.

"If you hear of anything," she said, "give me a call."

She settled up with the madam and left Jellybean Row to find a phone booth.

The hills were full of mansions and large private properties. Her only shot was to find this black coupe and follow it back to the nest.

"Baccalieu Cabs," the dispatcher said.

"It's Maria. I need Hank."

* * *

Aileen stroked the john's dark hair while he sucked at her nipple.

"Mama," he pleaded. "Mama."

"Shh," Aileen cooed. "That's a good boy."

He pulled away and lay flat on the bed. Aileen changed his adult-sized diaper. The john put on his suit and left. Shortly thereafter came a knock at her door.

"Come in," she said.

"Was that the diaper guy?" Roisin asked.

Aileen rolled her eyes. Roisin came in and sat on the bed.

"Is it true he sucks on your nipple," she continued with a grin. "Like a baby."

"I don't see what the big deal is," Aileen replied. "Some the girls get so freaked out by these sorts of fetishes. I think it's easy money."

"Oh, I'm just having fun. I have one regular who asks me to step on his balls and call him all sorts of names."

They both laughed at this.

"At least the weirdos know exactly what they want," Aileen said. "Sure, they do most of the work. 'Oh, you want me to just sit here while you jerk off onto my toes? Sure, no problem. Now, pay up.' The ones I have the most trouble with are the repressed ones who're too shy to ask for what they really want. I can never give them what they need. Then I get the lecture."

"It'll come in time," Roisin reassured her. "It's all about figuring out which character you're going to play. Once you learn how to give them something they never knew they even wanted, that's when you'll start making the real money."

There was another knock at the door.

"Come in," Aileen called out.

The madam opened the door. She was accompanied by a woman. Aileen and Roisin recognized her. It was The Woman.

"Leave us," Patricia said. Roisin left and the madam shut the door. "Aileen," Patricia continued. "We've met briefly before but weren't properly introduced. My name is Boudica."

She held out her hand. Aileen stood up to shake it.

"No, please, sit," Patricia insisted. "I'm sure you've had a busy evening."

Aileen struggled to find words.

"There's no reason to be nervous, my dear," Patricia said. She took up a brush and stood behind Aileen, combing her hair. "I understand someone came by here earlier tonight, asking questions. A private investigator named Maria Costa. Townie. Long black, curly hair."

"I'm so sorry," Aileen said, fighting back tears. "I didn't really tell her much at all. Just that a lady came by the brothels regularly and sometimes brought girls up to a mansion in the hills. I don't even know if that's true or not. She just wanted to know gossip and such."

"It's OK, my child." Patricia held Aileen's face in her hands. "I just needed to confirm what this Maria Costa knows, is all."

Aileen couldn't hold back her tears any longer.

"This was bound to happen sooner than later," Patricia explained. Her eyes began to shine. "In fact, I've been counting on something like this so we can take the next step. There are things set in motion now that cannot be stopped. It's more a matter of knowing the timetable. You have played an important role in an extraordinary series of events that are about to unfold."

"Can I come?" Aileen asked, tears all but gone.

"To the mansion?"

"Yes. Please."

"I'm sorry, child, but we have everyone we need now. I know your struggle. Believe me, I do. I know how you long to escape. Such sorrow behind your eyes. You have suffered like so many of our people. But soon we won't need a mansion. We won't need a sanctuary from oppression. Soon all of Baccalieu will belong to the Merrow once again. Now, I'm giving you the rest of the night off to rest your weary soul."

Patricia left and Aileen floated to her bed. She slipped into a restful sleep the likes of which she'd hadn't known since childhood.

* * *

"The missus has been on my ass about reno'ing the bathroom now for ages. I don't know what to be at with it and it's not like I can afford to hire a crew to come in. I tell her it's fine. The plumbing works, what else do you want? She's talking about home equity in case we ever want to sell. Are you kidding me? Took me ten years to save up for a down payment on a mortgage and you're already talking about selling. It's never enough. I never should've moved up to the plateau, see. Gave her delusions of grandeur, I think. Sure now she's talking about moving into one of the houses they're selling to Merfies just beyond the red line. What most Merfies don't understand, and I keep trying to explain to her, is that these aren't mortgages, they're 'on contract.' You know what that means, don't you? That means buyers don't actually own their homes until the mortgage is paid in full. Miss one payment and you're kicked out with zero equity to show for it. And y'knows them landlords are looking for any reason, no matter how small, to kick out buyers. Just another way Townies be sucking up wealth from Kildare."

It was 3 a.m. now. They'd been staking out Jellybean Row since 10 p.m. The air was coagulated from the pack they'd smoked between them. Maria drained the last remnants of whisky from her small flask, cursing herself for these slightest of restraints she imposed on herself. She had a suspicion that if this uber madam was going to show, it would be this time. The night was winding down and the girls' wills would be at their lowest after working a full shift. Not that they'd need much manipulating if Aileen was any indication. Or at least, she'd better show up because there were no more cigarettes or booze.

Sure enough, a black coupe pulled up, just as Aileen had described. A lady got out and went inside one of the brothels.

"Show time," Maria said, interrupting one of Hank's soliloquies.

The woman soon exited the brothel with a young girl following behind. Hank did his best to keep a tactful distance, but it was difficult to be inconspicuous on the lonely boulevard this time at night. It also wasn't very common to see cabs leaving Kildare to head for the hills at this hour of night, but this was Maria's only lead. It was easy to track the coupe's headlights as it swerved through the bending road. Maria could see the twinkling lights of massive properties shining onto their private ponds. The coupe eventually pulled off down a side road.

"What do you want to do?" Hank asked.

"Park a ways up and I'll walk down," Maria instructed.

She got out of the cab and walked through the wood surrounding the side road the coupe had taken. It was about two hundred metres until she reached an iron fence. The fence seemed to stretch out both ways to the cliffsides. The property must have been on the bluff overlooking the bay. Beyond the fence she could see men carrying flashlights patrolling with dogs. She walked towards the road and saw that there was a gate guarded by two men. A car was leaving the premises, exiting the gate. Maria got as close as she dared. The passenger in the back of the car looked familiar. She crept a little closer and hid behind a tree. It was Councilman Ferreira.

CHAPTER NINE

"I ain't afraid of no Boogieman," Iain called down to his mother.

He checked his hair in the mirror one last time then went to his closet. There was a loose tile at the back where he kept his stash, a brown paper bag filled with vials of heroin. He rolled it up and tucked it into an inside sleeve of his jacket.

Downstairs, in the living room, his little brother was sitting, reading comic books while their mother listened to the radio. Cian was passed out in the recliner with an empty bottle in his hand, as per usual.

"You better not be out there slinging," Iain's mother barked.

"Like you give a shit," he replied.

"What did you say to me?"

"I said, 'like you give a shit.' Who do you think buys his comic books and candy? Who bought that radio you're listening to? How do you think the ice box and pantry is magically refilled every week? Certainly not himself there on his throne."

"He's got a bad back!" she cried.

"Who said something?" Cian mumbled, stirring in his chair. He tipped up the empty bottle to his mouth then frowned when nothing came out. He fell back to sleep.

"If they catch you," his mother said. "They won't be sending you back to Agueda."

Iain shook his head then left. Throughout the whole exchange, Liam never looked up from his comic book.

He left his mom's row house on Ard Aoibhinn Ave. and made his way towards Ballybane Road. It wasn't a long walk and he enjoyed taking the time to get his mind right for the ten hours of work ahead of him. Or maybe less. The bag of heroin tucked into his coat under his arm might sell out quickly tonight. It was a warm Saturday night—always great for business.

Youngsters flitted in and out of brick tenements connected row upon row. Plywood and blankets covered smashed windows. Vacant lots were covered in graffiti and gutted by capers seeking any kind of copper that could be sold.

Iain found himself a nice little slip road to set up shop for the night. Either out of habit or nostalgia, he found a little crack in the small alleyway to stash his dope. Frenzied free radicals unhinged from any and all acceptable societal behaviours, the fiends bounced around the half-mile looking for product, deals, or anyone willing to share. Iain wasn't greedy with the local junkies. No need to step on the product or water it down or overcharge. Besides, word got around quickly enough among junkies.

Soon enough, a bow-legged fiend ambled his way. Iain thought he was peculiar because he twitched and shuffled like a regular junkie, and had that unmistakable hunger in his eyes, but he seemed too healthy. The customer mumbled something incoherent and thrust a few bills towards Iain, who straightened them out and examined them under the streetlamp. The money was right, so he set aside his suspicions. Probably a recovered addict who'd recently fallen off the wagon yet again. One of the things keeping Iain from the needle was that he knew it was a one-way trip; once you were a pickle you couldn't be a cucumber again. He pocketed his first wad of cash for the night then ducked into his alleyway to grab some product. Once the transaction was complete, the junkie crept off back into the shadows.

An expensive coupe pulled up beside him. The driver was a nervous Townie. Beside him was a pretty Merfie girl. Iain recognized her as someone he'd gone to junior high with, but couldn't remember her name. She smiled at him. Iain decided to raise the price by thirty percent.

"Seems like a lot," the Townie said.

"This is good shit, baby," the girl said and winked at Iain. "Worth the extra quid, believe me."

Not wanting to seem like a cheapskate in front of his date, the Townie ponied up. Unlike the fiend's money, these bills were crisp and clean. Iain gave him the product and the girl winked at him again before they drove off. Iain hoped he'd see her again soon and that he'd remember her name when he did.

This was what all those cops and counsellors didn't understand when they came to schools in Kildare to try to scare kids off the corner: if you were halfway competent with numbers, could dodge knockers and stick-up crews, and fight when you needed to, you could make double on the corner what fishermen made out at sea. It was a cold calculus no one wanted to admit. And as dangerous as Ballybane was, the sea was a lot worse. There were lots of kids in Kildare with fathers lying dead on the ocean floor.

After about six hours of work, Iain was doing his final count of the night, tallying up what he owed the mafia compared to the extra scratch he'd made juicing Townies, when he heard a familiar voice.

"Easy Iain," a woman's voice called out. That's what they called him in school growing up. He looked over and saw the girl he'd recognized earlier.

"Moira," he said, remembering her name now.

"I see you're out of Agueda."

"That's right. Making real money now, too."

"So I can see. You're not scared of the stories going around?"

"What? Some Boogieman snatching up dealers? Not a chance."

"Who do you think is behind it all?"

"Don't know, don't care. I'm just here to make money."

"I tried some of your product tonight. It's good stuff. What say we exchange services?" She stepped towards him as she said it. He could smell her perfume.

"Trust me, I'd love to, but I'm all out."

"That's OK. I accept cash, too."

Iain hesitated.

"Oh come on," she said. "You owe me for that sale earlier."

"Alright, you got me, girl. You got a place we can go?"

She led him to a row house a few blocks over from

Ballybane. The night sky was ripening to a dark blue as dawn approached. He admired her legs as she climbed the stoop up to her door.

"I hope you still have plenty of energy left after working all night," she said.

"Please," he replied. "You're going to be paying me after I'm through with you."

She opened the door and Iain was surprised to see the bow-legged fiend waiting in the porch. So surprised that he didn't have a chance to defend himself before the junkie cracked him over the head with a blackjack.

* * *

There was no more cringe left to overcome. No pimply college kids or skanky drunkards jerking off in a peep box. No paper mache coral reef or plastic fish dangling from dental floss. Instead, small table lamps twinkled in the dark ballroom like stars in the night sky. Wisps of cigarette smoke drifted throughout the room. A lone sax player from the big band started to play and Anne strutted out on stage, showing only her long toned legs beneath her feather fans. The spotlight illuminated her with a cone of light. The ballroom fell silent, aside from a few whistles and cheers whenever she teased them with a look at what was behind the fans. A long cigarette holder dangled from her lips. The drummer kicked the rest of the band off into common time and Anne tossed the fans. The crowd applauded. At the centre of the stage was a giant Absinthe glass and beside it a chair. A moody piano soloed over the band while Anne put her leg up on the chair to unclasp her garter. She pulled off her pantyhose and gloves to cheers and clapping. A raucous trumpet erupted while she untied her corset. She was naked now except for three expertly placed diamond triangles guarding her like armour. The band coalesced into a crescendo as she climbed the chair and into the Absinthe glass. She bathed in the frothy green liquid and the applause nearly drowned out the band. The music stopped and smoke crystal chandeliers hanging from the ballroom's ceiling illuminated the faces of rich Townie men accompanied by the Merfie girls on staff.

The curtains closed and she collected her stuff. Some of the men on staff pulled the martini glass off stage and prepared for the next show. Anne went backstage and dried herself off. She sat in her makeup chair wearing a robe and drinking a glass of water. As the adrenaline wore off, she was left with the same indelible image as always: the lusty expressions of all those Townie men in the audience. She wished she could think about something else, how the band sounded great and her feeling of joy in the moment, but she always seemed to fixate on the audience. They might have had more money, but they had the same bestial gaze as the men on Temple Street.

She took the staff staircase up to her room on the third floor. Just as she sat down to start removing her makeup there was a knock at her door. It opened before Anne could get up or say anything. Patricia entered holding a cup of tea.

"I loved your performance," Patricia said. "You're growing into a real dancer, an artist."

Anne didn't respond. She continued removing her makeup. Patricia laid the cup of tea on the vanity table.

"You don't agree?" Patricia asked.

"You and some of the other girls might get what I'm doing, but those men aren't much different than the mopes at Liban's. I appreciate that you've allowed me to create my own performance, but I still feel like I'm just a stripper."

"Drink your tea. Trust me, it'll make you feel better."

Anne took a few sips. The flavour was a rich blend of citrus, ginger, and cinnamon. Each mouthful brought a renewed sense of calm. The warmth from her belly spread out to her body, stretching all the way to the tips of her fingers and toes.

"Of course they don't get it," Patricia continued. "They're just a bunch of drunk old Townies. How could they see what you're trying to do?"

"And what am I trying to do?"

"You use humour to show that the outfit you're wearing is a costume. And when you're finally down to your nakedness, it's your humanity that's on display. The martini glass feels like a subversion of the mermaid trope. In a way, you're casting a spell, using illusion but calling attention to the illusion at the same time. Believe me when I tell you that when you're dancing, their attention is rapt. They may not understand what you're doing on a conscious level, but you're getting through to them subconsciously. I can feel it. That's the power of illusion. You've always had a knack for it. That's why you were so good at Inking down in the Gut. It's why I wanted you to come here and join us. We need people like you for our mission."

"Mission? What does that even mean? There's weird shit going on here that no one will explain to me." Anne sighed and rubbed her forehead. "I love it here, and I feel like I have everything I need, but I miss Kildare. I miss my friends and family. I don't understand why I can't leave and go home, even just for a day."

"You're right. I owe you an explanation and I'm sorry it's taken this long, but tonight I want to show you."

"Show me what? Just tell me."

"It's better if you see. Put this on and nothing underneath," Patricia handed Anne a robe. She put her hand up before Anne could interject. "Please, just roll with it for a little longer. After tonight, if you want to leave, so be it. But, first, finish your tea. I'll be waiting for you outside your door once you're ready." Patricia left the room.

Anne stared at the black robe and rope belt, still sipping her tea. Her anxiety melted away leaving only a sense of curiosity and anticipation. She got dressed and came out to meet Patricia, who was also wearing a robe and holding a wooden staff. At the top of the staff was a yellow gem held in place by gnarled wood carved into the likeness of tentacles. In her other hand she held an old tattered cloth sack that seemed to be holding a book. Patricia led Anne to the locked section at the back of the mansion. She took out a key from her robe and opened the door to reveal a large staircase. Anne looked down. The staircase descended far down into darkness. Sections of the walkway were illuminated by lamps. Anne could barely make out where it ended, but there seemed to be a faint glow emanating from the bottom. The silence took her breath away. Patricia began walking down the steps and Anne followed. As they descended, the heat quickly gave way, as did the light. The steel staircase weaved around the cave walls, spiralling downwards. Patricia walked with a steady, sure pace while Anne struggled to keep focus on her steps, gripping the guardrails firmly. For a moment she was lost in a pool of blackness and then the gem on Patricia's staff began to glow. Soon, a yellow glimmer appeared farther below. The stairs ended and they stepped into what appeared to be a cavern. The floor and walls were translucent onyx. Through the rock, Anne could see a kind of bioluminescence that bobbed around like small glowing fish. There were several tunnels branching off from this antechamber.

"Stay close," Patricia said. "Easy to get lost."

Heat emanated from the walls, too. A heat that pulsated, like the place was breathing. The gem on Patricia's staff pulsed in the same rhythm as the walls. The brief anxiety Anne had felt descending the staircase was gone and she felt increasingly euphoric the farther they got into the cave.

"After Colleen died, I was in a really dark place," Patricia said. "I blamed myself. It was my fault that she saw what she did. I tried telling myself that she knew the consequences of talking to police, but that was bullshit. And it wasn't just her death, either. I was dwelling on our constant state of poverty and felt like there was no escape from it all. I started taking long hikes in the hills to try and take my mind off of things. One day, I got real low and just wanted to curl up and die. I wandered around the woods until I came upon these caves. No one would ever find me here so I just lay down and waited for death. Once the pain of starvation and dehydration faded, I felt strangely euphoric, happy for the first time since Colleen was murdered. That's when I felt it calling to me. This place. The darkness was illuminated and I was led to this book." She held up the tome in the tattered bag. "I have learned so much of the secret history of not only our people, but the Indesejável, too. And more than that. It has given me power. Ever since that day, I've barely had to eat or sleep. I feel the power running through me at all times. This place has been the foundation of everything I've achieved these past few years."

Anne took in all this information with a bemused wonder. She knew it was madness, but the euphoria she was feeling helped her understand that it was a sublime madness. The cave's bioluminescence throbbed and grew to fill the entire tunnel with a golden hue that she could almost hear. The sound turned into human voices. They were chanting, chanting to the rhythm of the cave. She could hear drums. The further down they went the warmer it became. The tunnel gave way to a large grotto. People were dancing and chanting, swaying together in unison like wave upon wave. Anne could hear music, but couldn't see anyone playing instruments. Patricia slammed her staff on the ground and a loud crack shook the cave. Everyone stopped.

"Queen Boudica!" they announced.

"I have brought a new member to our family," Patricia intoned in a voice that was not her own. "Welcome Anne!"

Everyone cheered and the music resumed. Patricia gently pushed Anne towards the group. She approached slowly, tentatively. Someone grabbed her hand and pulled her in. The connection was instantaneous. Music filled her heart and she danced with a joyful abandon that she'd never experienced before. They revelled near a large pool of dark water. All light fled from it. Anne could sense a great power radiating from the water, but it was a dangerous power, one she couldn't hope to yield.

A loud crack from Patricia's staff interrupted the dancing again. The group turned their attention to her. A young man knelt beside her, naked.

"I have brought a sinner before you!" she announced.

"What are his crimes?" someone asked.

"Speak," Patricia said and nudged the man with her staff. He was bleeding and covered with welts. Anne could see now that he was probably only a teenager.

"I sold drugs," he said. "And...I hurt people."

"An apostate!" someone yelled.

"His name is Iain and he has confessed to me that he was employed by the mafia to sell drugs in Kildare. As contrition, he has offered the name of his supplier. He says he wants to join our family."

"He must be baptized!" someone else yelled.

"He must be judged by the Sunken King!" another yelled.

"So be it," Patricia said.

She pushed Iain forward with her staff. The revellers stepped aside and made a path to the pool. Iain hesitated. The water was still like a black obelisk. He put a foot in and gasped. He began to cry, barely able to control himself. Anne could feel the cold spread through her own body. He took a few more steps forward until he was in the centre of the pool, the water reaching his neck. The entire grotto rumbled and he was pulled under the water. Anne waited for him to come back up, but time stretched on and she couldn't imagine anyone holding their breath that long.

"The Sunken King lies dead but dreaming beyond the stars at the bottom of the sea, waiting to be woken."

The shining bioluminescence of the cave walls turned into twinkling stars. Anne felt the ground beneath her slip away and she was floating in space. The stars rushed towards her as she hurtled through the universe towards a giant rock. A planet. Hers. The land rushed towards her and she recognized the Gut, but there was no harbour or houses, just a sloping hill with trees. She crashed into the water and dove through the ocean. It was filled with fish that she didn't recognize. Ancient ancestors to what her people hunted. And then she saw Him. The Sunken King. Hundreds of knots of immense tentacles unwound to reveal a creature the size of a continent, too large for Anne to comprehend. She felt overwhelming sublimity that teetered between terror and jubilation. Before her mind broke trying to comprehend His geography, He opened his great yellow eye and she awoke. She opened her eyes and saw that she was back in the cave. Iain was standing at the edge of the black pool. Something had changed in his eyes.

"Queen Boudica," he said and knelt before Patricia.

"You have been judged," Patricia said. "And found worthy!"

Everyone cheered.

"Ph'nglui mglw'nafh Cthulhu R'lyeh wgah'nagl fhtagn" Patricia intoned.

The group repeated it, including Anne.

Despite having never heard the language before in her life, she knew exactly what those words meant.

CHAPTER TEN

"Who the hell are you?" Councilman Ferreira demanded. "How did you get past security?"

Maria entered Ferreira's office and threw an envelope on his desk, scattering pictures of him undressing his mistress. He picked up one showing him getting spanked with a riding crop. His leather chair creaked under his weight when he plopped down. After a few deep breaths he looked at Maria. She knew what he was thinking, measuring. Guys like Ferreira knew when to cut their losses.

"Alright," he said. "What do you want?"

"The mansion in the hills. Tell me about it."

Ferreira looked briefly surprised, like he was about to ask her how she knew about that, what was in it for her, then thought better. Maria was developing a weird admiration for him.

"It's a casino and brothel. Caters to the rich and powerful of Baccalieu. It's called Talamh an Eisc."

"Talamh an Eisc?"

"Some Merfie nonsense."

"Who runs it?"

"I'm not sure. A woman who calls herself Boudica seems to preside over it. The staff are all Merrow."

Maria handed him a picture of Anne.

"Have you seen this woman there?"

"Maybe. There's a lot of redheads there."

"She's a dancer. I'm told she's very good."

Ferreira took a closer look.

"Yes, she does seem familiar. I think she might do some burlesque performances."

"I want you to take me there."

"That's a bigger ask than you realize. They don't exactly allow dates. Boys only."

"That's fine. I'll hide in your trunk and find my own way in."

Ferreira again stared silently, measuring her up, weighing the risks.

"Who hired you to take these photos?" he asked.

"I don't think you're in a position to make those sorts of demands."

"I don't think you realize the seriousness of your request. If I'm caught trying to sneak you in then I'll be banned from the mansion, effectively cutting me off from all the big players in the city."

"Ramos."

"Ha! That dog. I knew it. What will you tell him?"

"That you're a hardworking, pillar of the community. All those late nights were constituent meetings after all. I'll even offer him his money back."

"When do you want to do this?"

"Now's as good a time as any."

Ferreira picked up the phone and called his driver.

* * *

After driving around in Ferreira's trunk for about an

hour, Maria finally felt it slow to a stop. The driver came around and opened it. She was dressed in black with a hood covering her face.

"If you're not here by the agreed meeting time, you'll have to find your own way back," the driver said. "We're not waiting for you."

She got out and found cover under some shrubs to observe the comings and goings of the mansion. Growing up in the east end of Baccalieu, Maria was used to seeing large properties, but she'd never seen anything like Talamh an Eisc. She could only imagine the wealth that generated it. What struck her most was that it seemed both modern and ancient. It was clearly a new structure, given the unworn state of the materials and grounds. But it also seemed to have always been there, like the land had formed around it.

Ferreira had explained to her that the third floor was the staff's quarters. That's where she'd need to get to make contact with Anne. She watched the windows but didn't see any activity. The halls were dimly lit on the third floor compared to the rest of the mansion. She noticed a large section at the back of the mansion where there were no windows. If she was going to find any trace of Anne she was going to have to get in there.

A guard holding a flashlight was doing rounds. Maria waited for her opportunity then ran around to the other side of the mansion where she found a staff staircase that opened to the outside. The door was unlocked. She ran up the stairs quickly, but the door to the third floor was locked. She got her lock picking kit out and set to work. It was a simple deadlock that would be easy to rake. As she slid her tension wrench in, she heard a door open at the bottom of the staircase and someone beginning to ascend. Maria kept her hands steady and jostled her pick until she felt all the pins were aligned. Whoever was below her had reached the second level and was still climbing. Maria opened the door and slipped inside, shutting it silently. In the hall, there was a small door, which she found to be unlocked. It was a broom closet. She slipped inside the dusty room and hid just as she heard someone cursing that the entrance to the third floor was unlocked. Footsteps ambled down the hall and entered a room.

Maria came out and put her ears to a few doors and checked their handles. When she found one that was empty and unlocked, she let herself in. The first thing she noticed was a large hooded robe laid out on the bed. Several footsteps were walking down the hall now. Maria opened the door a crack and saw a couple of hooded figures walking towards that section of the mansion without windows. It must be some place for convening. Her best bet for finding Anne was likely there. She donned the robe and caught up with the others. They were quiet and kept their heads down, so she didn't have any trouble blending in.

When they entered the section at the back of the mansion, Maria was shocked by the depth of the tunnel. But she was in too deep now to turn back so she kept going. They reached the bottom and began making their way through the network of tunnels. She struggled to keep from blatantly gawking at the translucent obsidian stone and darting bioluminescent lights. They were like a team of astronauts navigating wormholes through outer space.

Maria fetched her pack of smokes and started dropping cigarettes to leave a trail. When the tunnel broke into the grotto, Maria hung back. She found a side tunnel that brought her up to a bird's eye view. Beneath her was a large black pool that shone like an oil spill. She found its stillness unnerving.

More members trickled in. As the numbers grew they began to pass around a gourd, taking drinks from it. Some drums were brought out and they began dancing. They disrobed to reveal their naked bodies. That's when Maria saw her. Anne. Sean had told her she was a strong dancer, but that was underselling it. She moved like water. The group formed a circle around her and tried clumsily to follow her movements. A hypnotic effect even Maria couldn't resist started to take hold. The cave shimmered with the beat and the shadows transformed into monstrous shapes. Shapes of people blended together like a writhing beast flailing its tentacles. Maria caught herself leaning forward over the edge of the cliff, overcome with euphoria.

There was a loud bang that cut through the music and the dancing stopped. A woman holding a staff and a book addressed the group.

"Queen Boudica!" they cheered.

Before Boudica spoke she looked up to where Maria was hiding, smiled, then proceeded.

"I have brought a second offering to the Sunken King," she announced to cheers. "Tonight we take one more step towards ascension!"

A naked Townie man was brought out with his hands tied behind his back. Maria could see he'd been given a going-over, covered in cuts and bruises.

"Tell us your name and sins," Boudica demanded.

"Fuck you!" the Townie replied.

Maria recognized him as Nicolau Saraiva. Nico. A mafia thug who imported heroin. She'd know that horse face anywhere.

"This Indesejável represents one of the regimes that have corrupted and oppressed the Merrow," Boudica said. "No more!"

She pointed her staff towards the black pool. Two Merrow men grabbed each of Nico's arms, brought him over to the pool, and threw him in. Nico kicked and splashed, trying desperately to keep his head above water, but it wasn't much use without his arms. He soon submerged. Boudica read from her book in a language Maria didn't understand. The group repeated her phrases. The pool was still for a moment until a small circle rippled from the centre. A few more ripples. The water began to bubble. Maria could feel a small thud. Then another. It felt distant but approaching fast. The cave began to shake. The noise was coming from everywhere. Maria could feel it in her chest. Just when she thought her eardrums might finally burst, something emerged from the water. A green tentacle the size of an oak tree writhed, dripping with black ink. It stunk like brine. Everyone except Boudica got down to the cave floor in prostration.

"My Sunken King!" Boudica announced with her arms held open.

"The Sunken King!" everyone cried.

Maria could hear the sound of muffled cries coming from inside the tentacle. And then ripping and chewing until the crying stopped. The top of the tentacle opened like the teeth of a zipper and disgorged Nico's mutilated body. Maria fought the urge to vomit. The tentacle retracted back underwater. The pool rippled and was once again still as if only a small pebble had been tossed into it.

"Rejoice!" Boudica shouted.

The drums and dancing began again. Maria couldn't take anymore. She got up and started running. Her pulse throbbed in her head. She could hear the sound of her heart beating, louder than the drums. Her feet slipped and she fell down, beating her knees off the cave floor. She got up and started running again. The sounds of revelling were far away now. She slowed to a walk. Out of breath, she took a break to steady herself. A new panic crept upon her: she was lost. The caves all looked the same and she didn't remember how she'd gotten in. She started pacing around, trying to look for something that seemed familiar. A hooded figure appeared at the end of one of the tunnels. Maria stopped and watched. The figure walked away down another tunnel. Not knowing what else to do, she followed. When she got to the end of the tunnel, there was no sign of the figure.

"Maria!" a familiar male voice called out.

"Papa?" she whispered.

She spun around, trying to locate the speaker. The sound seemed to have come from the end of the tunnel, so she ran towards it.

"Maria!" a younger but also familiar male voice called, this time from the opposite end.

But she knew who that voice belonged to and it was impossible.

"What are you doing down here?" her brother asked.

"Still trying to prove to me that you're just as good as your brother?" her father asked.

The voices surrounded her, melding into a terrible duet.

"You couldn't hack it as a cop."

"The Gut is no place for sad little rich girls."

"Spoiled brat."

"All you're good for is taking cheques from other rich bitches."

"How many drunk men have you opened your legs for, whore?"

"You should've climbed inside a bottle and stayed there. Like your drunk mother."

Maria clapped her hands over her ears and started muttering: "Shut up, shut up, shut up. Shut up! Shut up! SHUT UP! SHUT UP!"

It was silent in the caves again. The sound of her voice echoed through the tunnels. She dropped her hands down and opened her eyes. Before her was the puffy, salt-white face of Colleen Gallagher. Maria fell to ground, crawling away backwards on her hands and feet.

"No, no, no, no," she cried.

The ghostly apparition marched towards her. It tried to speak but only scratchy gargles emerged. Brown water poured from its mouth. A scar as thick as licorice ran across its throat, ear to ear.

Maria's hand squashed something small and delicate. A cigarette. Another one a dozen feet away. It was the trail she'd left for herself. She scrambled up and followed it, never looking back to see if Colleen's ghost followed her.

CHAPTER ELEVEN

When Kieran saw Gaspar Reis' body a few days ago posed in that back alley off Temple Street, he thought it was the most fucked up thing he'd ever seen on the job. Certainly not the most grizzly thing he'd seen, but its macabre theatricality was unlike any gunshot wound to the face he'd come across. Now, looking at Nico Saraiva, he could see the bar had been significantly raised. The body was covered in that strange black tar again, but Kieran was familiar enough with Nico's equine facial features. Nico was posed on the bench overlooking the Gut that Kieran recognized as Maria's once favourite spot to talk with informants. He was sitting to the side, with his arm stretched over the back rest, head turned like he was talking to someone. That was strange enough, but on par with the Reis scene. What was really fucked up was that Nico had been sculpted to look like a mermaid. Sculpted. That was the best word Kieran could think of. Manipulated, moulded, carved, butchered. Incisions had been made into Nico's throat to look like gills. His back was filleted to expose a spine that had been cracked in three places to appear more dorsal-like. From there it only got more grotesque. His legs had been sewn together to resemble a tail. Kieran used the word "sewn" but he couldn't find a seam where the two legs should have met. He'd have to wait until the morgue washed off the tar before he could see what was really going on there. And, finally, there were the feet. Or rather, the caudal fin. Somehow, Nico's feet had been shaped to look like a giant fin. Kieran crouched down and examined the handiwork. Not only did the murderer(s) chop up Nico's feet and splay the delicate bones, but they also twisted them around, positioning the big toes on the outside, so the fin was a truly fish-like bowl instead of a bipedal arrow.

Patrolmen had formed a perimeter while a tent was erected to conceal the body, much good that it was. This time the press had been ready and were out in full force by the time Kieran had arrived on the scene. This was an open space, too—unlike the closed-off alley—so they couldn't keep them from taking photographs. At least the tent would shield the public once they appeared. Like Gaspar, Nico's body had been found by a fisherman heading to the Gut just as morning dawned. And, like Gaspar, the body had been left there without any sighting of whoever had done so. Kieran examined the scene for forensics using all his knowledge and focus but found nothing.

"Holy shit."

It was Martim. Kieran turned to face his partner and found Martim as pale as Nico was black.

"I guess you can call this escalation," Kieran observed.

"The poor bastard," Martim lamented.

"Don't feel too bad. That's Nicolau Saraiva. He had his share of bodies, although he never took such sadistic glee as whoever did this."

"Nico? How do you know?"

"I'd know that horse face anywhere. Well, seahorse now."

Martim was silent at that bit of gallows humour. Kieran realized that all of this must have been getting to him if he was being this unprofessional.

"I'm getting this to the morgue ASAP," he said. "Forensics will be here soon to scour the place before it becomes a zoo. I want you to piece together Nico's recent whereabouts quickly and get back to me."

"You got it, boss."

Martim took off with a purpose. Kieran only then realized that his partner had never removed his handkerchief from his nose. Kieran couldn't even notice the stink of brine anymore. He must have gotten used to it.

* * *

Kieran sat waiting in the morgue. The attendants had learned their lessons from Reis and were able to clean the tar off Nico much quicker this time. Kieran tried to rein in his impatience while he waited for any possible clues from the body. He heard a door open down the hall. It was Martim.

"Looks like you're probably right about Nico," he said. "I spoke to his wife. He didn't come home last night. I got in touch with some of his mafia associates. They were out at a restaurant downtown last night. Nothing crazy. They saw Nico get in a cab. I spoke with his mistress, too. She didn't see him either."

"Hold on," Kieran remarked. "You're telling me he hasn't even been missing for twenty-four hours?"

"He got in the cab around 10 p.m. last night."

"His body was found at around 5:30 a.m. this morning. How could they do that in only a couple hours?"

"Detectives." Dr. Chavas interrupted them. Kieran had never seen the coroner look so shaken.

"What can you tell us, Doctor?" Kieran asked.

"You're going to have to come look."

It was certainly Nico. Kieran had no doubt about that now that he could see his face. Beyond that, he couldn't believe what he saw. There were no scars or stitch marks to indicate where and how they'd managed to split and sew Nico's body to appear like a mermaid. The body was as seamless as when it was covered in the black tar. The skin was cleanly grafted.

"The body has been completely exsanguinated," Dr. Chavas explained. "The blood was probably drained through the slits in the throat. I have never seen anything like this before, so I can't begin to hypothesize how this mermaid effect was created without hours of examination."

"Here's another wrench, Doctor," Kieran said. "This was all done in less than six hours."

"Impossible," Dr. Chavas replied, now even more alarmed.

"That's the timeline we're working with," Martim confirmed.

Dr. Chavas reached into his pocket for a cigarette and left the room.

"What's our next move, boss?" Martim asked.

"I want to brace the Family," Kieran said.

"You want me to do that?" Martim asked.

"No, I think an uppity Merfie will put Don Ribeiro on his toes. You follow up on the cabbies."

* * *

"Do you have a warrant?" the guard asked Kieran, unimpressed by the badge.

"Tell Don Ribeiro it's about Nico," he replied.

After a short conversation in his booth, the gate retracted. Kieran drove down the highway flanked by poplars. The trees showed no sign of the oncoming fall; this late summer heat was keeping everything unseasonably green. There was a doorman waiting at the front of the property. He let Kieran into the Don's mansion and led him to a cigar room where Ribeiro and his consigliere were waiting. Kieran knew he wasn't going to be able to intimidate either of these men; he doubted anyone ever could. Don Ribeiro had gone legit so long ago that he needed only worry about tax attorneys. Kieran was going to have to push his buttons somehow.

"You get lost coming out of the Gut, detective?" Don Ribeiro asked.

"Like I told your friend at the gate, this is about Nico."

"What about him?"

"He's dead."

The consigliere glanced quickly at the Don, who remained impassive.

"How?"

"Homicide. The official cause of death is loss of blood, but that doesn't do it justice. He was butchered in a way I've never seen before in all my years on the force. Some real occult shit."

The old mafia Don leaned forward and put his hands on the table, fingers crisscrossed. His shoulders were slight now beneath his maroon cardigan, but the scars on his liver-spotted knuckles testified that he understood violence intimately. The cigar room's walls were populated by bookshelves full of textbooks on economics and history, but Kieran was sure the Don hadn't read a page. Probably his consigliere, but certainly not Ribeiro. He could try and disguise himself with as much sophistication as he liked, he was a thug nonetheless.

"How?" the Don repeated.

"He was butchered to look like a mermaid."

A single bead of sweat trickled down the Don's forehead. Kieran was right to have led with Nico. The old lieutenant's drug trade had buttered Ribeiro's toast for years, eventually providing him with the capital needed to catapult into legitimacy.

"Those animals," the Don muttered to himself.

"Do you have any idea who did this?" Kieran asked.

"You're goddamn right, I do!"

"Sir," the consigliere began but was cut off by the Don.

"I'm not going to help the pigs do their work," the Don said. "Especially not no Merfie pig."

"Give me a break. If you know who was behind this you would've taken them out long ago. Nico had lost control of the Kildare market. I'm seeing less politicians and business types hobnobbing with the Family these days. Looks like you still got some fight in you, but I'm guessing not the muscle. I'm not going to bust you on drugs or racketeering. I'm here about the bodies. Talk to me."

Kieran could see in the Don's eyes that he'd love to demonstrate just how much fight he had left in those old meat hooks. Ribeiro controlled unions, waste management, construction contracts, the shipyard, and who knew what else. He was almost seventy years old. But that was never enough for people like Ribeiro. They always wanted more.

"You're right that someone cut him out of the Kildare drug market. Right under our noses. That's fine. I didn't mind. Nico had taken that for all it was worth and was ready to retire. But then we started losing friends. Whoever was doing this was starting to gain profile, too. Cutting in on our contacts. So I had Nico start pushing product on Ballybane again, if anything, to provoke a conflict, flush out our enemy's main guys."

"Did you find out who was behind it?"

"Just whispers and hearsay. A lot of superstition. You know how your people are."

"Humour me."

"Something about a 'Boudica' and mansion on the hills."

"'Boudica?'"

"Yeah, whoever is leading this operation apparently likes to call themselves that."

"Themselves? Is this Boudica a man or woman?"

The Don shrugged his shoulders. Kieran knew this was far more than he could've hoped for, so he'd cut it there.

"Thanks for your time," he said, making for the door.

"Don't get used to it. I ain't no snitch. This is only on

account of my old friend Nico. The next time you show up at my gate you better have a piece of paper or a SWAT team."

Kieran made his way out. Whoever this Boudica was, they'd managed to intimidate the mafia into cooperating with the police.

* * *

Kieran met Martim in the office parking lot.

"Any luck with the cabbies?" he asked.

"No," Martim replied. "No cars missing. I spoke with all the drivers who were on shift last night and none of them recognized Nico."

"If the car isn't missing that means it wasn't jacked. The cab must have brought Nico to the site. Probably in on it."

"What about Ribeiro?"

Kieran recounted his experience with the Don.

"Boudica, huh?" Martim asked. "Think it's legit?"

"Best lead we have right now. The only one."

Kieran got to his desk and found a note from the secretary that Maria had called him. He recognized the callback number as Sean Gallagher's. He dialed it.

"Hynes!" Maria said.

"What's going on?" he asked.

"I found Anne. She's involved in some kinda cult. There's a mansion up in the hills. All kinds of weird shit going on. I'm pretty sure they're responsible for the disappearances, too. I saw them kill Nico. I recognized prostitutes and dealers and gang bangers there. Whatever they're doing it seems pretty fucking big."

"Whoa. Slow down. Your voice is trembling. Are you OK?"

"I saw something. I don't know, maybe it was just some weird trick of the sound and the shadows. Those caves aren't like anything I've ever seen."

"Caves? This is getting pretty crazy."

"You don't have to tell me. Get a team together. The whole goddamn squad and raid that mansion. And if you go down into the basement... into the caves... be careful."

"You know we can't just raid a place like that with-out—"

"Just do it! And fast. I don't know if it's a mass sui-cide or if they're trying to start some kinda revolution, but whatever they're planning, it's happening soon."

"Was there someone there named Boudica?"

"Yes! She's the leader!"

"OK. I'm on it."

The line went dead. Kieran sat at his desk and stared at his phone for what seemed like hours. Everything Maria said added up. How could she have known about Nico and Boudica otherwise? Besides, he trusted her more than anyone beside his wife. Maybe even more. He got up and went to Major Cardosa's office.

Kieran knocked on the door softly. "Mind if I have a word, Major?"

As per usual, Cardosa looked at him with mild annoy-ance and pointed at one of the two chairs in front of his desk with his pen. Kieran sat down.

"I have a lead on the murders and possibly the miss-ing persons, too," he said.

Cardosa raised his eyebrows.

"An informant told me there's a mansion in the hills where there might be some potential cult activity. Seems like these missing people are either joining or are being used as some kind of sacrifice."

Cardosa's pen briefly paused when Kieran mentioned "mansion in the hills" then resumed its rhythm. When Kieran finished talking, Cardosa chuckled quietly.

"A cult," he said and laid the pen down on his desk.

"I know it sounds outlandish, but this is the biggest break we've had in months now and it might be worth following up on."

"The only break you've had, you mean," Cardosa said. Kieran was silent and waited for the Major to continue. "I'm familiar with the mansion you're referring to. And I can guarantee you that there is no such thing going on." Kieran was about to reply when Cardosa smiled and stood up. He walked around the desk and sat in the chair beside Kieran. He tapped Kieran on the shoulder — the only gesture of comradeship he'd ever shown. "You're a good officer, Hynes. Exemplary. I don't have to tell you how much good you've done for your community and the profile of Merrow such as yourself in this department. And I hear you've finally started a family. A young daughter. Now, I'm going to let you in on an exciting opportunity. The Deputy of Ops is opening up and I'm taking it. But keep that to yourself. Sergeant Da Luz will be taking over as Major here at Homicide. Which means someone needs to take over Sergeant. I'd love to put your name forward. I think you'd be an excellent candidate. What we need for you right now is to show the people that we've done everything we could to track down these missing persons.

It's the sad truth that as far as Kildare has come, there is still so much work to do. It's important that everyone in all of Baccalieu sees that we are holding the line on this path we've forged. To lose public trust now would be to undo all the great work this department has done. It'd be a shame to see that happen and for you to lose the great strides you've made in your career. Not just for yourself but for all Merrow. Do you understand what I'm telling you?"

"Yes, sir," Kieran replied. "But we still don't have any other leads on these killings or disappearances. And these occult killings are escalating."

"Gaspar Reis and Nico were criminals. The public will soon recognize that and opinion will turn. It seems to me that you've done an excellent job on this case. Keep up the good work."

"And the mansion?"

"I tell you what. I'm going to personally look into it and I'll follow up with you immediately."

"Thank you, sir."

"Good lad." He patted Kieran on the shoulder again and went back to his desk. "Shut the door on your way out, please."

Once Kieran was out of the office, Major Cardosa picked up his phone and dialed Commissioner Neto.

"We have a problem," he said.

CHAPTER TWELVE

Before Maria knocked on Sean's door, she tried to balance herself. The door, the hallway, and the entire world swayed like a tiny dinghy atop choppy waves. The journey from Talamh an Eisc to a payphone in Baccalieu was a formless blur without time. After she managed to follow her cigarette trail out of the caves, it was a mad reckless run from the mansion out onto the road where she hitched a ride with a trucker. At some point it had started to rain overnight. Buddy must have had some experience with picking up panicked women on the side of the road because he was smart enough to keep quiet and not ask any questions once he saw the look on Maria's face. She could remember her hands shaking as she plugged in Kieran's number and left a message with the secretary. On the walk over to Sean's, she'd tried to gain some composure, but it refused to come. Sudden noises startled her and in every innocuous shadow something seemed to quiver. Unbidden, images of that great tentacle invaded her mind. Not just its unfathomable size, but the stench, too. Like something that had been rotting for a thousand years. It was something ancient and dangerous, far beyond the instruments of humans. She couldn't think about it because if she did she thought that she might go insane. A drink, she needed something to drink. Just a little something to calm her nerves. No. She was going to have to stay sober to explain this to Sean. After that, she would allow herself a drink. Several. However many she wanted, needed.

He opened the door and looked her up and down, dripping wet from the rain. Maria entered without waiting for him to invite her in.

"Whisky," she said.

Sean pointed wordlessly to a small wooden cabinet in the living room. Maria opened it and saw that it was full of expensive stuff aged in cork barrels floating in a pond of milk and honey populated by water nymphs for a hundred years. That sort of thing.

"Do you mind?" she asked.

"Help yourself," he answered.

The first shot didn't even register. The second one tingled going down her throat. The third warmed her body. After the fourth she was ready to sit down and talk. This really was good stuff. She grabbed a second glass and handed it to Sean.

"You're going to need this," she said.

He obeyed without protest.

"Your sister is wrapped in some fucked up shit," she said.

"You found her?"

"Yeah, but the trouble is gonna be getting her out."

"Why? What's she involved in?"

"It's like some kinda cult."

"Cult?"

"I tracked her down to a mansion in the hills. Talamh an Eisc."

"Talamh an Esic? That's Merrow for 'land of fish.'"

"Not the time for a linguistics lesson, Professor."

"Yes, of course, sorry."

"On the surface, it looks like a gentleman's club. There are some big players involved. Politicians and business-men going for gambling and women. But the place is run entirely by Merrow. They seem to live there, too. I followed a group of..." Maria searched for the right word "... worshippers down into a basement that led into a cave. And there..."

"What? What did you see?"

Maria took the bottle of whisky and filled her glass. She handed it back to Sean and gestured he do the same. He took a small mouthful. It wasn't enough. Nothing would be enough for what she was about to tell him.

"They killed someone. A Townie drug dealer. Nico Saraiva. Mafia. Know who that is? No? Doesn't matter. They threw him in a pool of water as part of some kind of ritual sacrifice. They were dancing around naked and a woman was leading the whole thing. She was reading from a book in a fucked up language I didn't recognize. It wasn't even Merrow. Then the cave started to shake. And..." she drank straight from the bottle this time. "...a tentacle came out of the pool. This thing was the size of a fucking tree, I'm telling you. They called it the Sunken King. It spit out Nico. The guy was mutilated. Like some-one had moulded him like putty. After that I ran, hitched a ride, and came here."

Maria wasn't sure how she'd expected Sean would re-act, but she certainly didn't expect him to be excited.

"Amazing," he said finally. "The book is real."

"Of all the crazy shit I just told you, you're interested in a book?" Maria responded.

"In my research, I've come across mentions of a text that was lost in the caves above Kildare. After a devastating storm a long time ago, affluent Indesejável wanted to destroy it, like they blamed it for everything that had happened. The sense I got was there were dark rituals and conjurations going on."

"So you believe me? I don't even believe myself. I feel like I'm going crazy."

"I can't explain what you saw. All I can say is that this cult activity fits within a larger historical framework."

The phone rang. Sean, who didn't get many calls, looked at it like he'd forgotten he even had a phone.

"That's probably Hynes," Maria said and answered it. After speaking with Kieran she sat back down.

"Did you say the leader's name was Boudica?" Sean asked.

"Yeah. Why?"

"That's interesting. When the Indesejável first started repressing Merrow, a woman named Boudica resisted. She led a failed rebellion to try and drive them out. After it failed they jailed her and she hung herself. Or poisoned. There's different apocryphal legends."

"So she's a history buff. Maybe the two of you would get along."

"Do you think the police will raid the mansion?"

"I don't know what they'll do. I suspect the commissioner is probably tied up in it, too, to be honest."

"I could try to get in and make contact with her."

"No offence, Professor, but you're not exactly their clientele. Hynes is our best bet."

"He was certainly right about you."

"He has his moments."

"I see there still aren't many female officers. Much less detectives. Seems like it's still very much a boy's club."

"That's putting it nicely."

"Is that why you quit?"

Maria was silent.

"I'm sorry. I don't know why I tried to be coy like that. I know it had to do with Colleen. It's still really hard to talk about it directly."

"I saw her in the caves last night, too," Maria said after a drink.

"What? Colleen?"

"I think it was the place trying to fuck with me. Like it could see inside me and dredged up all the shit I try to keep buried. I heard the voices of my father and brother, too. Did you know I had a brother?"

"No, I didn't."

"Why would you. Luciano was his name. Luke. He was such a golden boy. My parents adored him. And so did I, the little shit. Everyone did. He was handsome, smart, a great athlete. All my little girl friends loved to come over to my house and swoon over him. Especially when he was in the pool. He loved to swim. All of my dad's partners and friends called him the Anointed One. He was going to take over the family business and carry the Costa dynasty to new heights. And if he felt any pressure, he never showed it. That's the worst, you know. He just handled it so well. He wasn't a brat like me. More than anything, though, he loved to fish. We had a boat that he'd take out for deep sea fishing, catching marlin and swordfish. Mom still has them mounted at the house. Then, one day, he and some buddies got caught out there in a storm and drowned."

"I remember hearing about that," Sean said. "It was a pretty big deal. I'm surprised I didn't connect the dots."

"You probably assumed I didn't come from the rich Costas. Well you can imagine what my house was like after that. My family fell apart. Dad was a workaholic, my mom an alcoholic. I became a clichéd rebellious shithead and did everything I could for their attention. After high school, my grades weren't good enough to get into college, but there was this big push to get more women into the BAPD. So I applied. Now that pissed my parents off. I can remember the recruiters. They must have thought I was perfect. A sad little rich girl out to prove something to her parents. I'd wash out soon enough and I'd be their alibi for why women didn't belong in the force. But guess what? I was pretty good. No, why am I being modest? I was really fucking good. I was a great cop. Soon enough I was in the criminal investigation division and then homicide. In Kildare of all places. Everything was going great until..."

"Colleen."

"She was going to be our star witness. She was a nurse. Young, just starting out. Hard worker, kept her nose clean, her head down. Just wanted to make a life for herself. Not too much to ask, is it? Anyways, she was in the wrong place at the wrong time. The suspect was a guy we were trying to nail for years and her testimony would've tied it all together. But she was scared. Everyone is scared in

Kildare. No one talks to the police because no one wants that snitch handle. It's a death sentence."

Maria wasn't sure why she was recounting the details of a case that Sean was intimately familiar with, but it was like a reel in her mouth that she couldn't stop from unspooling. Sean seemed to understand this and did not interrupt.

"But Hynes wanted to change all that. The first Merrow detective and he was a great one. Still is. Probably the best. Anywhere else in the world and he'd be the goddamn commissioner at this point. Not Baccalieu though. But he was preaching to anyone who'd listen that this was our chance to make a real difference. That if we all worked together we could bring these guys to justice. The killers, the dealers, the gang bangers. Finally bring some peace to the Gut. And I was hooked. I believed him, every word. He converted me. His specialty was talking to the young guys. I was good with the women. So I came to Colleen and converted her, too. Told her to 'be strong,' that it was 'the right thing to do,' that together we could 'change the community.' All that bullshit. And then...they killed her. Not only did they kill her, they tortured her, raped her, mutilated her, and dumped her in the Gut for everyone to see. After that, I was done. It broke me. Before that, see, I could put up with all the bullshit. Not just the sexism for me but also the racism for Hynes. It was worth it because we were gonna change everything. The department, the city, everything. After that, I realized we weren't changing anything."

And then it hit her. All the pain that she'd been holding onto burst forth in a wave of tears. She sat on the couch and wept. Sean came over with a wool blanket and wrapped it around her shoulders. She leaned towards him and he held her while she cried. After it was all out, she felt totally drained. Her body went limp, the extent of her exhaustion now apparent.

"Lie down," he said once she stopped sobbing.

She was too tired to argue.

* * *

She woke up a couple of hours later. Sean was on the other side of the couch reading. It was evening now. She'd slept through the entire afternoon.

"How are you feeling?" he asked.

"Better. Thanks. Do you have any coffee?"

Maria followed Sean into the kitchen where he brewed a pot. She opened the cupboards and passed him a blue mug and grabbed a yellow one for herself.

"I'm sorry," he said. "I hate to do this, but that's Anne's. She always insists on using it when she comes to visit and makes me promise not to let anyone else use it. I know it's weird, but it's a sibling thing."

"Oh no, I totally get it."

She put it back and grabbed a different one. They drank together in uncomfortable silence. Maria took in the details of the apartment for the first time since arriving as a nervous wreck this morning, which now seemed like a lifetime ago. It was small and simple, not a lot of possessions aside from bookcases lining the walls. She noticed several mermaid sculptures. They weren't arranged decoratively, more so an overflow of research material.

"I can be a little exhaustive with accumulating research material," Sean admitted when he saw Maria looking around.

"Can I ask a dumb question?" she asked. "Why mermaids? Or Merrow. The whole thing. Did we actually think you people came from the sea? Seems kind of dumb."

"I'm not sure how literally the first Indesejável colonizers took this belief, but it definitely came from seeing us worshipping sea people. We'd offer sacrifices to the merfolk and in exchange they'd provide us with the fruits of the sea. Also, fishermen believe that merfolk will rescue the faithful from drowning should they fall into the waves. There are all kinds of folktales and songs about people who claimed to have been saved by merfolk and heard their songs. People used to believe the merfolk taught us music. Of course, the Merrow are simply a personification of the sea, which dominated our lives. It still does. But that's a pattern consistent with all peoples. In the Old World the Indesejável used to believe in forest and agricultural spirits until they became more secular."

"What if they're real?"

"What do you mean?"

"What if the merfolk are real? If what I saw last night was real then merfolk could be real, too."

"Yes, that certainly complicates things." Sean took a few sips of coffee. "I remember coming across a very strange text during my undergrad. A kind of grimoire. I can't remember the title of it now. At the time I dismissed it as the ramblings of a delusional mystic. I think the author's name was Abas, or Abdul, Aljazeera, or some such thing. Anyway, it posited that there were a superior race of beings, gods essentially, who ruled over the universe, and that all our mythologies were attempts at representing them. I suppose that mad mystic might have been onto something after all."

Maria finished her coffee and continued to poke around at some of the mermaids.

"I apologize for the state of the place," Sean said. "I spend most of my time on campus, either at the library, in class, or my office. I really just use this place to eat and sleep. And house extra junk."

"Aren't you lonely?" Maria regretted asking the question immediately after the words left her mouth.

Sean seemed more surprised by the question than wounded. Like he'd never really considered the possibility of loneliness and was now shocked to discover that he did indeed suffer from it.

"I live a monkish lifestyle," he said. "And I've been unwilling to compromise to accommodate another person's needs. I won't lie, there have been many times at the pub near campus where I've been tempted by a young grad student, but that's exactly the kind of excuse the university would love to use to fire me."

"What about Kildare? Do you have any friends or family that you still keep in touch with?"

"Not really. Aside from the perfunctory calls to my parents, I only really had a regular relationship with Anne."

He sighed.

"When I first asked you to find Anne, you asked me why I didn't invite her to come live with me here in town," he said. "I gave an evasive answer. I guess the truth is that, deep down, I held her responsible for Colleen. Certainly not directly, I mean to say. Indirectly. That Anne participated in the lifestyle that keeps Merrow down and creates the circumstances for someone like Colleen to be murdered."

He paused to drink some coffee and consider how he was going to phrase what came next. He set his cup down and picked up a wooden mermaid sculpture.

"It's funny," he said. "My life's work is about dismantling that exact belief but not even I can rise above that sense of resentment. Goes to show how deep our internalized racism is."

Maria took the mermaid from Sean and laid it back on the shelf. She held his hands in hers.

"I'm going to get her back," Maria said.

She saw his seafoam green eyes quiver behind a sheet of water. They pulled closer to each other. She smelled the coffee, tobacco, and aftershave from his body. His hands gripped hers, gentle and firm. When she felt the involuntary movement of neck craning towards him, she pulled back.

"I should go," she said.

"OK," he said.

"Thanks for everything."

Before she left, she took one last look at him thumbing through some texts on a bookshelf then closed the door.

CHAPTER THIRTEEN

Commissioner Neto sat across from Patricia, being boring as usual.

"I knew you were up to some weird shit with this place," he said. "We were happy to turn a blind eye while you did what you had to do to get the streets under control. But this is too far. You're fucking with citizens now."

"Reis and Nico were both drug dealers and criminals," Patricia countered. "What you really mean to say is Indesejável. You were fine when it was just Merrow."

Neto smiled.

"We allowed you to take over the drug trade in Kildare from the mafia because you promised us low homicide numbers" he said. "And you delivered. Business has been good and everyone is benefiting. Why mess with a good thing?"

"You 'allowed' me? As far as the drug trade is concerned, the mafia is just a couple of malcontent Townie boys playing thugs. The real power players went legit years ago. Their sons and daughters are lawyers, doctors, and business owners. Real pillars of the community. But that's the nice thing about being a Townie. Even if you're excluded from power at birth, you can thieve your way into it. Money is money in Baccalieu. Not true in Kildare."

"Yes, it's all very unfair. But that's the world we live in, unfortunately."

"Not for long."

"What are you talking about?"

"Your time on this stolen land is at an end. The real custodians are taking it back."

Patricia stood up from her desk, perused her book shelves, then came over and sat down on the couch with Neto.

"I can offer real justice, not the cruel oppression you and your kind have been using to keep us subjugated. The Sunken King will soon wake to cleanse this city in a tidal wave of blood and anoint me as the rightful queen."

"You've gone insane."

"For a while I thought so, too. But everything the Sunken King promised me has come true."

Her eyes began to glow yellow. Neto maintained his dismissive smirk until he felt the pressure of her gaze. Blood leaked from his nose then ears. He collapsed on the floor convulsing, holding his head. He looked up at Patricia, pleading her with his eyes, begging her to stop the pain. His mouth opened, but he could only groan. He stopped then and lay still.

Patricia slouched into the couch with her arms and legs outstretched, neck bent backwards in a position of profound weariness. That was the most she'd ever stretched her powers and she now felt exhausted. Her mind raced and anxiety began to take hold. She was suddenly overwhelmed by the enormity of her mission. All those sleepless nights, all those hours scouting prostitutes and drug dealers, all those tedious conversations with politicians. And for the first time since she was near death in the cave nearly five years ago, she felt doubt. Not only about whether she could achieve her lofty ambitions, but whether they were as righteous as she'd always assumed. No. Not the first time. Some part of her mind had remained untouched by Him. She looked to the small safe in the corner of the room where she'd sneak documents when the occupied part of her mind wasn't paying attention. It was a paper trail. For who, she didn't know, but some repressed part of her knew she ought to leave something behind.

She fell to the floor beside Commissioner Neto and crawled towards her desk. The book, she needed the book. She reached up to her desk and swatted it down onto the floor. The book landed on its spine and spread open. Its text glowed with a yellowy shimmer. Patricia read and felt its energy enter inside her. She closed her eyes and meditated, taking a few deep breaths. Her racing thoughts slowed and the burning anxiety in her chest abated. When she opened her eyes again, she felt like she'd slept eight hours. Able to stand now, she rung the bell on her desk. Yeti entered with his bow-legged strut and Iain at his side. They looked at Neto's body then to her in questioning alarm.

"He's not dead," she said. "He must be fresh for the Sunken King. Take him down to the cave. And bring me Anne Gallagher. We must ready ourselves for the end-game."

Yeti and Iain carried Neto out of the office. A few moments later, Anne entered.

"I have a very important mission for you," Patricia said. "I need you to bring your brother here."

"Sean? What do you want with him?"

"The pieces are just about set for my ascension. He must be present."

Patricia saw the fear in Anne's eyes.

"Don't be afraid. It will be a joyous occasion. This is what all our hard work has been leading to."

Patricia resumed her meditation. She was going to need a lot more energy for the next twenty-four hours.

* * *

Sean was sitting on the couch staring at the wall. He'd been there ever since Maria left after breakfast, smoking his pipe. Thinking through things like this was a slow burn problem, which required a pipe. And tea. Coffee made him too jittery for reflection. Coffee and cigarettes were for grading and deadlines. A pipe and tea were for quiet contemplation.

He'd never heard of this "Sunken King" in his research of Merrow lore. The Merrow never participated in blood magic until the Indesejável arrived. Before then the Merrow would make burnt offerings and build effigies with shells and fish bones on the shore for the merfolk then perform rituals involving dancing and music. The merfolk were more or less benevolent and would bless the Merrow with bountiful fishing seasons if the rituals were properly performed. A "Sunken King" that demanded blood sacrifices in order to bestow some sort of violent power or deed seemed out of character for the Merrow.

He took a puff from his pipe. The smoke was thin so

he tamped it. As he was exhaling a long plume of tobacco, a knock came at the door. It startled him and he began to cough. He got up from his chair and opened the door. Anne was standing on the other side.

"Can I come in?" she asked.

Sean silently stepped aside and let her in.

"Granddad's pipe," she observed. "You must have been deep in thought. Sorry for interrupting you."

Sean was still silent. Anne looked at his mug on the table.

"Could I have some tea?" she asked.

He went to the kitchen and poured some tea into her favourite mug and brought it into the living room. She was sitting down on the couch. Sean sat across from her.

"I'm sorry to barge in on you like this," she started. "You must have been very concerned about me. Please accept my apology for all that."

"I don't care," Sean said. "I'm just happy you're safe. Listen, I know about the cult, the mansion, and the rituals and everything."

"Boudica said you probably would."

"Boudica. Who is she?"

"Patricia Powers."

Sean spit his tea out. "Patricia Powers is the cult leader who seized control of the Kildare underworld?"

"You keep saying cult. But it's not a cult."

"I don't want to argue with you. All I want is for you to be safe. This group you're involved with are tapping into some very dangerous...I don't even know how to describe it. But the police know about it and they're going to shut it down soon. Just stay here with me and ride it out."

"They can't stop what's about to happen. No one can."

"What's about to happen?"

"I can't explain it in words. You'll have to meet with Boudica."

Sean knew he was being led into some kind of trap. Patricia, or Boudica, wouldn't have sent Anne unless she was trying to manipulate him. Despite her play being patently obvious, it carried with it a powerful trump card: more than anything, Sean was powerless against his own curiosity. He had to know if it was all real. He had to see it. He had to see that book.

They stood up and left the apartment. Sean left the door unlocked.

* * *

The pages were unsettlingly smooth, not fibrous or paper at all. Was it skin? Sean wasn't sure if he was ready for the answer to that question yet. It was bound by two wooden boards sewn with tough sinewy threads. The text was written in some kind of hieroglyphic alphabet that he didn't recognize. What disturbed Sean most was that this book was supposed to have been lost for hundreds of years, and yet, it showed no signs of damage. But it was also undeniably ancient, too. While it would have to be examined by an expert, he didn't doubt its authenticity. There was power in this book, he could feel it.

The door opened. It was Patricia. Or Boudica.

"That language is the closest approximation two-dimensional text can come to the tongue of the Old Ones," Patricia explained as she entered her office.

Sean was sitting on a cigar chair holding the book.

"The Old Ones?" he asked.

"The gods who rule over all reality," Patricia said and smiled.

"I see. You're very trusting to let me hold it."

"A learned man such as yourself wouldn't dream of damaging so precious an artifact. Besides, there's nothing you could do to damage it."

Feeling its latent power in his hands, he didn't doubt that was true.

"How can you read it?" he asked.

"It revealed itself to me," she answered. "Take your time. It may do the same for you."

"And this book showed you how to become a crime lord?"

"I wouldn't say it's a how-to guide. It imbued me with its power. His power."

"The Sunken King?"

"Yes."

"Tell me how you did it. How did you take over Kildare's black market?"

Patricia seemed bored and disappointed by the question. She leaned back in her chair and puffed her cigar.

"I started with the working girls. They're the most vulnerable, as you know. After that I brought some of the lower-level dealers into the fold. The next step was to start eliminating the bigger, more violent players. Some of them joined me, most of them served as sacrifices to grow my bond with the Sunken King. Once I'd knocked off the gang bangers without bloodshed, I got the police on board to allow me to move in on the mafia's territory.

They folded without so much as a whimper. At that point I controlled just about all the drug trade and prostitution in Kildare. I used the money to build this mansion and started bringing Baccalieu's politicians and businessmen into my orbit. The real gangsters."

"The recent sacrifices. Why the escalation, the theatrics?"

"To sow chaos. The Sunken King thrives on it."

"But how did the book help you?"

She smiled at that question.

"I can't explain it to you in words. You'll have to open yourself up to it and see for yourself."

"I can't read it. I don't have a codex."

Patricia didn't answer and simply nodded at the book. Sean opened it and started at the beginning. He stared at the symbols trying to discern some kind of pattern. The edges of the red letters started to shine with a yellowy glow. Sean heard a voice in his head. Not a voice. A hum. It swelled in his mind until a profound sense of euphoria consumed him. He started flipping through the pages and he understood. When the Indesejável first arrived and learned about the Merrow's rituals, they married it to their own will to power. It was no longer about communing with the earth so that she may share her riches but about dominance. Sean felt the Sunken King's power. He knew that if he gave himself over he wouldn't need to worry about sleep or sustenance. He would never tire. Boundless energy. He could read the university's entire library and publish rows of books and papers. He'd be the greatest scholar on the continent. The world. He would be a philosopher king.

"Your work was instrumental in helping me understand my role," Patricia explained. "It helped me understand how the Indesejável have subjugated our people and how that has led to endless misery and suffering. Like Colleen. And now you will play an important role in the final sacrifice. Tonight, we will offer Commissioner Neto to the Sunken King. This will bring the full force of Baccalieu's power upon us. When the time is right, you will sacrifice me to the Sunken King so that I may ascend to become his queen. Together we will rule this land as its rightful heirs."

She was right. Sean knew it. The Indesejável were trespassers. They needed to die. It was only right. After all the violence they'd done to the Merrow. It was only right they be eliminated and the land given back to its rightful owners.

He shut the book.

"No," he said. "Don't you see what's happening? You're retreating into our worst, primal instincts. Worse, you're combining that with the Indesejável's will to power. This is vengeance. I want to build a better society, too. But not one built on bloodshed."

"It's not enough to describe the state of things, you must change them. You'd rather be like Kieran Hynes? Working within the system? Slowly pushing that rock uphill only for the trespassers to roll it down every chance they get? It's time for radical action."

"You're not talking about change, you're talking about annihilation."

"You're afraid."

"Yes, I am. You ought to be, too. I don't think you understand the terms of the deal this Sunken King is offering."

"Perhaps a demonstration is in order."

* * *

Sean stood beside Yeti and Iain who held an unconscious Commissioner Neto. Patricia proselytized before the dark pool in her strange language. Behind them, Anne led the procession in a revelling dance. Sean was strangely proud of his sister. But mostly sad that this was the only way she could've discovered her full potential as a dancer. He turned his attention back to the pool. It emitted a terrible power.

Patricia finished her sermon and pointed at the pool with her staff. Iain and Yeti carried Neto into the water and dropped him then promptly retreated. The grotto shook. Everyone got down to their knees and prostrated themselves except Patricia and Sean. Just as Maria had described, a giant tentacle emerged from the water and disgorged the mangled body of Commissioner Neto. Sean stared at the body. Two more tentacles of equal size emerged from the water.

"Kneel if you want to live," Patricia advised.

Sean dropped, vaguely aware of the shocking pain in his knees from striking rock. A hum filled the grotto. It was a low grumble, but he could detect the occasional shift in pitch. The Sunken King was speaking to them.

"The time has come!" Patricia announced. "The final stage of our plan will now be set in motion."

The cultists revelled.

"Only one more sacrifice is needed." Patricia smiled,

looking to Sean.

In her hand she held a ceremonial dagger.

"You may not be the one to draw my blood," she said. "That's no matter. But you will be present for my ascension."

She turned her attention to her followers.

"The time is near! The Indesejável will try and stop us. They will loose their dogs upon us, but we will turn that against them. When the BAPD arrive, the Sunken King will feast, gathering the energy He needs to level this cursed city. Then we shall rebuild as the rightful rulers of our land!"

Dancing and music followed. The tentacles squealed with what Sean thought was hungry anticipation. They quivered and retracted back underwater.

CHAPTER FOURTEEN

It had happened like the other two. They got the call at around 5 a.m. and estimated it had been placed there sometime between then and 4 am. The difference now was that instead of a drug dealer or Mafioso, this was the police commissioner. But, unlike the other two bodies, Neto wasn't covered in black tar. Whoever did this wanted everyone to know who the victim was. But Kieran knew who did this. Boudica.

Kieran stared at the mangled body of his boss. Neto was bound in between the statues of the Townie and Merrow fishermen in the red line near Intersticio. His flayed limbs were spread out and extended to emphasize his squid-like form. Using his knowledge of human and squid anatomies, Kieran deduced that Neto's humeri had been removed and reattached to his femurs from the knee down with his feet fitted to each humerus to form two tentacles. The ulna and radius of each forearm and the tibia and fibula of each leg were split to form eight legs, extending from his hips and lower abdomen.

Kieran and Martim, along with every available homicide detective, worked briskly to gather evidence before the scene turned into a circus. A crowd of Townies and Merfies had already accumulated outside. Patrolmen held them back from the scene. It was only 7 am. In another hour there would be a mob. By 9 am, they were going to have a full riot on their hands. Kieran stepped outside the tent. The sky was full of hard grey clouds and the air was thick with humidity. Flashes from photographers' bulbs were like lightning strikes. A storm was coming.

"What do you think?" Martim asked. He looked as tired as Kieran felt.

"We're going to have to get his body out of here before the fireworks start," Kieran answered.

The medical team bagged Neto, lifted the body onto a stretcher, and wheeled it out of the tent.

"Good riddance," someone shouted in a Merfie accent.

"Hey, fuck you!" someone shouted in a Townie accent.

Some pushing and shoving ensued. Patrolmen intervened to keep it from escalating. Kieran hoped that moving the commissioner's body as soon as possible would help to diffuse this crowd, but he doubted that would work. The situation was boiling over now. He could feel it. It was in the air. The long humidity that had been simmering for weeks had broken. It was time for some thunder and lightning.

He got into his car with Martim and they followed the ambulance as it left Kildare towards the city morgue. A few people banged on their car. Patrolmen tried to keep them away. They slowly made their way out of the growing mob. Angry people were flowing into the red line from both Baccalieu and Kildare. The ambulance pulled off into the morgue, but Kieran kept driving.

"Where are we going?" Martim asked.

"To get answers," Kieran answered.

When they got to the precinct, Kieran headed straight for Major Cardosa's office. Martim tagged along until Kieran held his hand up to let him know that he didn't want his partner in any part of this. Martim was smart enough to get out of his way.

The major was on the phone. Kieran swung Cardosa's door open so violently it shook the wall.

"I'll have to call you back," he said when he saw Kieran. "What the hell do you think—?"

Kieran grabbed Cardosa by the collar, hauled him up off his chair, and shoved him against the wall.

"Tell me about the mansion," he growled into the major's face.

Cardosa looked up at Kieran. He was probably a full foot shorter. All the old condescension had drained away from his face to reveal what had always lain underneath: fear. Kieran realized then that Cardosa had been afraid of him his whole time at homicide, clinging to their power imbalance as a shield. He wasn't just afraid of Kieran's size and power, but what he represented, too. Change. The unstoppable force of change. Kieran threatened to usurp all the mediocrities in Baccalieu. Cardosa must have understood on some level that he was an endangered species. All these guys did. That's why they fought against guys like Kieran. And Maria. And Sean. To keep their jobs, their positions, their influence. Kieran felt delirious at this realization, almost drunk with a new sense of power. He fought to keep control.

"I told you about that place and you said you'd look

into it," Kieran said. "Now the commissioner is dead. Talk, goddamnit!"

"It's a brothel where the big players go," Cardosa said after some hesitation. "Whoever runs it has taken over Kildare."

"Boudica," Kieran interjected. "Who is she?"

"I don't know her real name, but all the prostitution and drugs run through her. She's got everyone in her pocket. It also helped keep crime down in Kildare, so the commissioner was happy. The politicians, too!"

"And I'm sure everyone got a taste," Kieran said.

"Of course. They were behind getting rid of the gang bangers. But no one thought it would turn into whatever is going on with these murders."

Kieran released Cardosa who collapsed to the floor rubbing his neck.

"You had me on a wild goose chase," Kieran said. "You knew where all those missing people were, but you had me running around wasting time. Just so you could show the Merfies you were doing something. You set me up to fail."

Cardosa was still on the floor trying to catch his breath. He didn't have an answer for Kieran.

"I want any available officers who aren't dealing with that shit show at the red line right now," Kieran said. "I'm going to raid that mansion and rip this Boudica out root and stem."

"You got it. Whatever you need. Anything."

He left Cardosa's office and went to his desk to call Maria.

"Hello?" she answered.

"We're hitting the mansion right now. I could use your eyes."

"You're going down into the caves?"

"If need be."

There was a long pause.

"I don't know, Kier," Maria replied. "I'm just a civilian now. I'd only be getting in your way."

"I understand," Kieran said.

"Good luck."

Kieran hung up the phone and got to work.

* * *

A riot isn't just a collection of individuals; it is a process. A group of people don't gather with independent desires to break windows. Someone or something has to start the chain reaction. In a group large enough, by law of average, there will be at least one person who is perpetually one inch away from beating the shit out of something. A threshold of zero. Something triggers this person and they go off. Then, another individual, who is always itching to beat the shit out of something but needs a little push in the right direction (a threshold of one), sees the first guy go off and they want to join in. And so on until now the old lady who runs the local flower shop is throwing gas bombs at cop cars.

That's what happened when the League of Indesejável Supremacy showed up. Frederico Da Rocha led his army of skinheads to the scene at the red line at around 9 am. By that time, the place was full of both Townies and Merfies, hurling insults at each other. There was some pushing and shoving but no real aggression. Then the League appeared. Da Rocha couldn't have picked a better moment to make his appearance. The mob was at a precipice. The police might have been able to pull them back from that ledge, but the League pushed them beyond the point of no return. A Merrow patrolman gave Da Rocha a gentle shove, a League crony punched the cop, and then mayhem broke out.

Police tried in vain to separate brawls. Fearing for their safety, the nightsticks came out. Then the guns. Bricks and stones smashed shop windows and the looting began. The humidity finally broke and the rain came hard.

* * *

Maria hung up the phone and lit a cigarette. She cursed herself for being such a coward. Kieran and all those cops needed her. Anne needed her. But she couldn't go back down into that cave. The only thing more terrifying than that giant tentacle, and whatever else was attached to it, was the thought of seeing Colleen's bloated face again. She fished out another cigarette before the first one was halfway finished. Her hands shook so much that she dropped her lighter.

"Fuck this," she said, then left her apartment.

Outside her building she could hear the riot going on near the red line. Smoke was rising through the rain. She walked westward until she found a cab that brought her to Sean's.

"It's me," Maria announced when she knocked on his door.

There was no answer. She knocked again. Still no response. She tried the doorknob and it was open. She wandered around Sean's empty apartment. There was a lingering scent of rich tobacco. Two mugs sat on the living room table with cold tea. One of them was yellow.

"Anne," Maria said out loud.

She rushed to the phone and dialed Kieran's desk. "C'mon c'mon c'mon," she said between each ring.

"Kieran," he said after picking up.

"I'm coming with you," she said.

"Glad to hear it. I'll come get you shortly."

"I'm at Sean's."

"I don't have to tell you that he shouldn't come."

"He's already there."

"What?"

"I'll explain on the way."

Maria waited outside Sean's condo building smoking a cigarette. Kieran's car pulled up with Martim in the passenger seat. Maria dropped the butt on the pavement and rubbed it out with her shoe then got in the back. Kieran introduced his old partner to his new one.

"I hope you have more than just the three of us," she said.

"There's a squad going up ahead of us," Kieran explained. "We're going to meet them there. I'll be leading the raid."

"What can we expect once we get there?" Martim asked Maria.

"They have a lot of old gang bangers kicking around so they'll have muscle. Otherwise it's mostly women. Prostitutes, dancers. They all seem pretty dedicated to the cult, so they might put up a fight, too."

"What else?" Martim asked.

"What do you mean?" Maria asked.

"Kier said you told him something about the caves shaking."

Kieran tightened his grip on the steering wheel.

"Let's just say we can expect some weird shit," Maria answered.

"What exactly are they trying to do anyway," Martim asked. "What's their goal?"

"Sean says it has something to do with an ancient god that lives at the bottom of ocean," she explained. "It caused the flood hundreds of years ago that nearly wiped out Baccalieu."

"Let's hope it doesn't come to that," Kieran said.

He turned up the volume on his dispatch. The riot in Kildare was getting worse. All available officers were being called to try and bring some order to the chaos.

Reading his thoughts, Martim said: "You made the right call bringing a squad out here. We'll put an end to this right now."

Maria didn't think it was going to be so simple.

They caught up with the retinue of police cars coiled around the empty road leading towards Talamh an Eisc. The gate was open and no one was guarding it. When they pulled up outside the mansion in the lot, the place seemed all but deserted. A silhouetted figure of a woman shifted behind the windows above the mansion's entrance. The officers got out and crouched behind their cars, guns trained on the doors and windows. Others ran around the back of the mansion, forming a perimeter. Kieran grabbed a megaphone from the trunk of his car.

"Boudica!" he said. "This is the BAPD. We have the

place surrounded. I have a warrant for your arrest. Come out with your hands up."

The figure didn't move. Kieran checked his watch and after a minute without activity from the mansion, he gave everyone the signal to approach the doors. One of the officers stood by with a two-handed ram, ready to bust it down, but it wasn't needed as it was unlocked. Kieran, Martim, and Maria all ran up to Patricia's office. It was empty.

"How did she get out of here so quick?" Martim asked.

"Must be a secret exit somewhere," Kieran speculated.

Maria suspected something more spectral.

They investigated the office until a SWAT member entered.

"We searched just about the entire place. No sign of anyone."

Maria could hear a faint throbbing. Below her feet she felt the floor vibrating.

"They're down in the caves," she said to Kieran.

"Everyone on me!" he called out, then said to Maria: "Lead the way."

Maria didn't need to follow her trail of cigarettes; the cave's bioluminescence led the way.

"They're leading us into a trap," she said.

"Probably," Kieran agreed. "But we don't have much of a choice."

The further down they went, the louder it got. It was deafening, impossible for a group of people to make this level of noise, no matter their number. The noise reached a thunderous clamour just as the tunnel broke into the grotto. Suddenly it was quiet. No one was dancing or shouting. They all stood there waiting. Patricia stood near the pool. She held a knife to Sean's throat. He was kneeling beside her, bound and gagged. In her other hand she held a book. Anne stood nearby.

"Drop the knife," Kieran shouted, pointing his gun at Boudica.

The rest of the officers pointed their guns at the cultists. No one seemed intimidated. Maria read the fear in Sean's eyes. He nodded. She knew what he was telling her: *It's real. It's all real.*

"Whatever you do," Maria said to Kieran. "Don't shoot her." She turned to Patricia. "Just let the people go. We'll escort anyone who wants to leave."

"There's no getting away from this," Patricia said. "It's far too late for that. The Sunken King will rise. He will bathe Baccalieu in blood and we shall all be reborn as the rightful masters of its land and sea."

She raised the blade to Sean's throat in a tearing motion. The cave echoed with the sound of a gun firing. It was Martim's. He shot Patricia in the forehead. She grinned and stepped backwards into the pool. Maria ran towards her to stop her from falling, but it was too late. Patricia dropped the book and blade and fell into the water. Black droplets splashed and her body quickly submerged. There was an unearthly silence in the cave. Maria ran to Sean and untied him.

"We need to get out now!" he cried as soon as Maria pulled out the gag.

The cave began to shake.

* * *

The *Esmeralda* gamely climbed the choppy waves. Captain Neves struggled to see through the rain pouring over the wheelhouse windows. They were two hundred miles from shore and the weather was only getting worse.

"There wasn't nothing like this in the forecast," the chief mate observed.

"In my thirty years, I've never seen anything like it," Captain Neves replied.

Waves kicked up frothy water onto the *Esmeralda's* deck, rocking her back and forth. Her seasoned crew fought to keep from vomiting down in her quarters. They looked out the porthole and watched as the grey sky turned dark and mean. The sun was obscured by clouds filling the sky with streaks of blue lightning. As the *Esmeralda* bounded another swell, the captain and chief mate saw something that rendered them speechless. A one-hundred-foot wave rose before them like a mountain, reaching towards the sky.

"Impossible," Captain Neves muttered.

He drove the *Esmeralda* into the beast as hard and fast as he could, climbing towards the wave's summit. The crew shouted and cheered as she neared the crest. But the apex continued to recede before them. Unable to breach the fulcrum, the *Esmeralda* tipped backwards and was swallowed whole by the sea.

* * *

In the cave under Talamh an Eisc, three tentacles emerged from the water, dripping with black water, filling the cave with the stench of brine. The cultists got down on their knees, rejoicing with tears in their eyes. BAPD officers gazed at the writhing limbs, their guns trained nowhere in particular. The tentacles peeled open to reveal row upon row of teeth.

"Fall back!" Kieran commanded.

It began to feast. The tentacles made no distinction between officer or acolyte, Townie or Merrow. Some cultists held their arms open in welcome as the tentacles plucked them up from where they stood. Others lost their nerve and began to scream, trying to escape. The police unloaded their revolvers and shotguns into the tentacles, their bullets barely piercing the creature's hide. Occasionally they'd hit one inside its mouth and would blow off some hunks of flesh and shards of teeth, but even that did little to slow its feasting. The muffled cries of its victims being eaten alive joined the cacophony in the cave.

"Fall back!" Kieran repeated over the chaos.

Police followed him as they walked backwards towards the exit, their guns still trained and firing upon the tentacles. Cultists fled with them.

Maria ran to Sean and helped him to his feet.

"Where's Anne?" he asked.

Maria looked around and saw Anne standing near the black pool, staring at the tentacles like a shell-shocked soldier.

"Anne!" Sean cried.

She looked to him with confused and sad eyes. The cave shook, loosening heavy rocks. A boulder fell in front of Anne, knocking her back into the pool. There was a splash and she was gone. Without hesitation, Maria sprinted to the pool and dove in after her. Sean was about to join her when someone grabbed him.

"What are you doing?" Kieran asked. "We all need to get the fuck out of here."

"Anne and Maria are down there!" Sean screamed.

Kieran looked at the black pool where the tentacles writhed. Sean was looking in the same direction and he saw it: the book.

"You get as many people out of here as you can," Sean said. "I have an idea."

Kieran hesitated.

"Go!" Sean pleaded.

Kieran joined his police and whatever cultists they'd managed to rescue. Sean approached the book. Beside it he saw Martim Santiago's body, his head caved in by a rock. Sean took Martim's bloody revolver and pointed it at the book. He fired. The bullet bounced off it like it was made of solid rock. He flipped it open and fired at the pages. The bullet bounced again. He looked around and saw the ceremonial dagger Patricia had been holding. When he thrust it into the pages, the dagger splintered into shards in his hand.

The tentacles were growing larger. Soon they would fill the entire cave. Guns were firing and people were screaming. He got up and was about to leave with the others when he saw on the cave floor a hooked tooth the size of a banana from one of the tentacles. He grabbed it and raised it above his head like a dagger. The book's text then began to glow and the tentacles stopped their assault, their attention now focused on him. Sean felt the full influence of the book's seductive power. It invaded his mind with visions and promises of becoming a philosopher king. His loyal subjects admiring him, awaiting his decree. Above him, a tentacle slowly descended, ready to devour. Saliva dripped onto Sean's shoulder, disrupting the book's spell. He plunged the tooth into the pages, tearing through the text. A terrible scream pierced his ears. The tentacles writhed in pain. Burning hot ichor oozed from the puncture Sean had made in the book. The tentacles retracted back underwater and for a moment everything was silent. Then the cave began to shake even harder than before. Rocks crashed from the ceiling. Someone grabbed him by the collar and pulled him up.

"We have to go," Kieran said.

"What about Anne and Maria?" Sean demanded.

Kieran shook his head and dragged Sean back to the tunnels.

"No!" Sean screamed, but he couldn't pull himself away from Kieran's hold.

* * *

The riot continued despite the heavy rains. Angry people soaked to the bone threw bricks into shops and fists into faces. BAPD used their nightsticks to give wooden showers. The riot moved from West Baccalieu into Kildare where the mob pulled apart wooden buildings, shattering glass and homes.

No one seemed to notice the pool of water accumulating at their feet, rising inch by inch. Not until a four-foot wave rose from the Gut and knocked people to their knees. That got their attention. They turned to the sea and saw a great mountain of water rising. A blue and green monster of salt topped with raging froth. Waterspouts rose to the sky like great columns. This apocalyptic vision brought screams and cries full of panic and despair.

"The plateau!" people started screaming.

Merrow and Indesejável alike made a mad sprint uphill. They fought through the water, kicking up debris. Former adversaries picked each other up and continued the march, splashing through dirty water.

They reached the plateau and watched as the streets of Baccalieu and Kildare swelled with water. Cars and trucks careened into each other. People gathered at the tops of buildings. Everyone was watching the same thing: the giant wave threatening to drown everything beneath it. The entire coast went dark under its shadow. The people held each other, sure that death was now upon them.

Then, just as the wave was about to crash, it deflated. The water poured through the city then receded back into the sea, like a bowl being tipped to the side then returning to level. Above, the rain slackened then quickly dissipated before a radiant sun. The people fell to their knees, thankful for whatever miracle had prevented them from getting wiped off the map.

* * *

As soon as Maria dove into the water, the black coldness took her breath away. She couldn't see Anne; she couldn't see anything. The only thing she could sense was the tentacles' tectonic movement all around her. Then she saw it. The Sunken King. A great lidless yellow eye, a mass of bioluminescence hovering in a yawning abyss. Forms moved and writhed inside its mass; hands reached out through its surface unable to escape.

It was pulling her towards it now. She kicked her feet and paddled with her arms, but she couldn't fight its gravitational pull. Only a few feet away now, she could make out a face inside the yellow mass. It was Patricia. Her face vacillated between pain, sorrow, and ecstasy. Maria couldn't look anymore. The vision was going to drive her mad. She shut her eyes. But what she heard was even more disturbing. It was the sound of digestion. The shucking and dripping of stomach acid and bile as the Sunken King consumed its victims, body and soul. Maria nearly relinquished her last grip on sanity when a shrill wail pierced her. She opened her eyes and saw that the Sunken King's eye had burst. Streams of golden ribbons billowed from the wound. The great mass shook back and forth in agony. A vacuum opened in the blackness and the creature escaped into it. Maria was left in blackness. She realized then that she was drowning. Panicked, she tried to swim up towards the cave, but she couldn't find her bearings, aimlessly floating around in space.

Before she lost consciousness, she felt something attach itself to her face. A jelly-like substance slid inside her nose and mouth. She clawed at this foreign invasion until she realized that she could breathe. It was still too dark to see anything, but she felt movement. Her body was being guided. Cold strong hands held her against a humanoid torso with a fish's tail. Panic started to rise inside her chest once more. Then she heard it. A song. No, a lullaby. It guided her to sleep.

CHAPTER FIFTEEN

Maria opened her eyes and found herself in a room she didn't recognize. A harsh light above her made her squint.

"It's OK," a familiar voice said. "Take your time."

Her eyes adjusted and she could see that she was lying in a bed. She stirred and tried to sit up, but her body was as weak as a kitten.

"Here," the voice said, holding a straw to her face. "Drink."

The tepid water flowed through her body with a rejuvenating wave. She had the strength now to sit up and consider her surroundings. This was a hospital. She was lying in a hospital bed wearing a gown. There was an IV drip attached to her wrist. She turned away from the harsh fluorescent bull lights above her and saw that it was night outside. She was able to sit up, but her body felt like a slab of concrete and it took all her strength. Sean Gallagher was sitting to her right.

"What can you remember?" he asked, offering her more water.

"I remember going down into the caves," Maria said. "Then, a light? I was underwater. Someone saved me, I think. There was singing."

"Singing?"

"How long have I been out?"

"Well," Sean said, shifting in his chair. "That's a bit of a complicated question."

"How long?" she repeated.

"About two weeks."

He gave Maria a moment to digest this information.

"What's the complicated part?" she asked.

"You weren't discovered until about a week after the incident at the mansion."

"What do you mean? Where was I?"

"One morning some fishermen found you washed ashore in Kildare. No one knows how you survived so long in the water. You must have been trapped in some kind of pocket in the caves and then finally got sucked out into the harbour."

Maria was quiet for a while then, her mind stubbornly blank. The impact of this information combined with the haziness of her mind paralyzed her. A thought flashed and she shot up in bed.

"Anne!" she cried. "What happened to Anne?"

Sean was quiet. His chin fell to his chest and his shoulders trembled. He looked up and shook his head. Maria's face trembled and she pounded her fist against her thigh.

"A lot of people have paid a terrible price," he said. "But, the good news is that this may finally be the tipping point for Baccalieu. Kieran led an investigation into the mansion. He discovered a damning paper trail in Patricia's records."

"Patricia?" Maria asked.

"Boudica. Her real name was Patricia Powers. She was

actually Colleen's friend."

"Yeah, I remember her name now from Colleen's case."

"She was corrupted. Not just by the Sunken King, but by her feelings of grief and anger. It's curious that she left such exhaustive records. It's like a part of her was still in control and knew this was all for naught and that the real change would happen in the aftermath with evidence. Anyway, Kieran blew the whole thing wide open. He exposed all the connections between the BAPD brass, the politicians, and the mafia. Not like anyone really doubted these existed, but to see it all laid out like that is too incriminating to be swept under, even in Baccalieu. I doubt things will just improve overnight. There's plenty of anti-Merrow opportunists trying to pin this all on Kildare. But a few heads have rolled. Kieran is now the homicide major so that's a start."

Maria grinned to herself. Kieran homicide major.

A doctor appeared in the room with a nurse.

"I'll let you rest," Sean said, standing up to leave.

"I'm sorry," Maria said. "I promised you I'd save her and I failed you. Again."

"You did everything you could," he said. "When I saw you dive in after her, I..."

He leaned over and kissed her forehead then paused. They looked each other in the eyes. He turned around and left.

The nurses took her vitals and asked her questions while the doctor explained the rehab process. Maria stared out the window, unable to process anything anyone was saying to her. The stars shone brightly through the cloudless night sky. She fought to remember what had happened to her. Her mind groped through cobwebs until she wandered around a dark cave and was consumed by a yellow light. The stars swelled in the sky, threatening to leak in through the window. Panic overwhelmed Maria.

"It ate them!" she screamed. "It fucking ate them all!"

The nurses fought to hold her down while the doctor punched her arm with something sharp. A golden warmth filled her body and she relaxed into it, falling through her sheets and into a flexible and happy darkness.

* * *

Movers were busy hauling away the contents of Maria's old office. They carried out sofas, desks, and banker boxes full of documents. One guy busied himself with removing the door with the pebbled glass bearing Maria's name. Maria watched the men working closely.

"Are you in charge around here?" someone asked.

Maria turned and saw Kieran approaching her from down the hall.

"Sorry," she said, turning to face him. "I'm currently restructuring and not taking any clients at the moment."

"Does that mean you're looking for a new job?" he asked.

"If you're trying to get me to come back to the force, Major Hynes, you can forget it."

Kieran laughed.

"So you're moving out?" he asked. "Where's the new digs?"

"West end. That's where the action is. So they tell me."

"What about your secretary?"

"Had to let her go, unfortunately. This is going to be a more streamlined operation. Needed to cut my overhead."

"What are your plans for this place?"

"I'm renting it out. Going to need the money to supplement running a private investigation practice in West Baccalieu."

"It's a shame," he sighed. "You're natural police."

"It's not the work," Maria said. "It's the job. The badge. That's you. Not me."

"I hear you. You won't be making the kind of money you did helping rich housewives of East Baccalieu, but at least you're where the real action is."

"Mom always wanted me to do more volunteer work."

"Well, if this promotion thing blows up in my face, I might be asking you for a job."

"I highly doubt that."

Kieran smiled and leaned against a wall.

"Oh just come out and ask," Maria said.

"I just wanted to check in and see how you're doing," he replied.

"You mean after spending six months in the loony bin?"

Kieran didn't speak.

"I still can't remember much," she said. "To be honest, most of my time in the asylum was for getting off the booze and dealing with my family bullshit." She shuffled some papers then paused. "It's all a blur. That time I was missing, those weeks in a coma, and then the months of rehab. I get flashes, but it's hard to tell what's real. Like trying to remember a nightmare. The doctors figured I was better off just forgetting. "

"I know what you mean. Sometimes I'm not sure if what happened was real."

"What I don't understand is that no one is talking about it. It's like everyone decided to pretend there wasn't a goddamn monster down there."

Kieran winced when she said 'monster.'

"Cognitive dissonance," he said. "The same thing people did when they ignored all the stuff going on with the Gut. Out of sight, out of mind."

"Seems like people are looking now," Maria said. "I guess it's easier to acknowledge systemic prejudice than ancient gods waiting to wipe us off the face of the earth."

"I wouldn't hold my breath on that either. The BAPD have made a few high-profile promotions to Merrow like myself, but we'll see if that comes with a real commitment to better policing. There's still lots of rats on the force."

"You'll get them."

It was Maria's turn to be quiet now.

"Oh just come out and ask," Kieran said.

"Have you been talking to him?"

"A little bit. He's doing OK. Asks about you. Wants to give you space and all that. I tell him he's an idiot. Typical egghead. You should call him."

"Maybe I will."

"Well," Kieran said, getting ready to leave. "Just wanted to check in on you, kiddo. I'm sad I can't convince you to come back, but I'm sure you'll do well with whatever you do next."

"You taught me a lot, Kier," Maria said. "But I realize now that I didn't learn the most important lesson you tried to teach me."

"What's that?"

"It's about people. Helping individual people. Bringing justice to victims and their families. When I joined the BAPD I thought that if I couldn't fix my family then I could fix Kildare. I was thinking too big-picture, not seeing the forest for the trees or whatever. I was just another stupid tourist. But I can't help people as a cop like you can. I see that now."

"I thought you were supposed to be off the booze," Kieran replied.

Maria rolled her eyes.

"Get the fuck out of here," she said.

Kieran then embraced her. She felt like a child in his big arms. She hugged him back and they held each other like that for a while. Kieran let her go and strode out without saying another word. Maria smiled to herself.

She left her building and got a cab to the west end. The movers had all her stuff lugged into her new office. From her window she could see the Gut. Half-finished buildings stretched upwards, reaching with fingers made of rebar. It was a strange sight to see Kildare filled with cranes, cement trucks, and steel.

She tore off a strip of red tape and pasted it to the floor, outlining the floor plan for her new office. As she was measuring out where her couch would go, a pair of brown Oxford shoes appeared in her doorway. Above them were the tweed pants belonging to Sean Gallagher. She stood up and they considered each other.

"You have a grand view of the new harbour," he said without moving forward. "I used to resent all that wood as just another example of our subservience to Baccalieu, but to be honest with you I kind of miss it now."

"I'm just glad they didn't bother to replace that awful statue by Intersticio," she said.

"Speaking of which," he said, stepping over the line of red tape. "Care for a drink?"

"Sorry, I'm all dried out these days and that place would be a little tempting."

"Oh, right, I'm sorry. I should've known better."

"That's alright." She walked past him and held the door for him. "Why don't we go to your place for some tea?"

END

DARK STORIES FROM ENGEN BOOKS

THE HOWL BECONS

Growing up without his father, Tyler had no way of knowing the horrible secret that has plagued his family for generations. To free himself and find the cure, he will have to look beyond himself and into his dark history.

"A very ambitious novel... the horrors of everyday life can be worse than anything in fiction. The idea of using werewolves as a metaphor – to me this pushes the book a bit above much of what is out there... Brad [Dunne] is a very good writer and obviously has a deep background."
— Andrew Peacock

WESTON'S WAR

Something evil grows in the heart of Colorado. Bill Weston was a man of the West. He knew it – its land, its people, its stories. It was where he plied his trade, hunting men for money. His life wasn't easy, but it was predictable. That all changed when he captured Faraway Sue and he was led on a trip through the Colorado forests

"Take a little Zane Grey. Add a little Penny Dreadful. Read with Sam Elliot's voice. Discover Jon Dobbin's masterful The Starving."
— Darrell Power, Great Big Sea

ON SALE NOW FROM ENGEN BOOKS

"Dunne breathes life into a world of magic and lore that will draw the reader in right up to the epic conclusion. Ashes is a heroic tale not to be missed."
Amanda Labonté
bestselling author of Supenatural Causes

When fifteen-year-old Phoenix loses her caregiver, everyone that she has ever known inexplicably turn their backs on her. Given the impossible burden of repaying an unknown debt, Phoenix sets out on her own with her trusty donkey, Muler, as her only companion.A chance encounter with Malcourt, a mysterious traveller, not only saves her life, but sets it on a trajectory that she would have never thought possible.

THE XANDER DREW SERIES

Prologue: The Long Road (May 2014)

COMING SOON FROM ENGEN BOOKS:

FATE'S SHADOW

A violent past case is reopened as Xander must contend with Detective Thomas Horton, the vigilante Shadow Flame, and a returning figure from his youth in Coral Beach -- all while trying to prevent a murderer from running free. Can Xander stay the course even as his world crashes in around him?

The early years of **Xander Drew** as he struggles with the evils of his small rural hometown of Coral Beach, Maine. Cursed with the heart of the Womb and the gift of seeing the world around him for what it really is, Xander must learn the hard lessons about the nature of humanity to traverse the minefield of criminals, gangs, and abusers that stand between him and ultimate happiness -- but most of all that **sometimes it takes a monster, to catch a monster.**

"THE WRITING OF ITS GENERATION- - VISUAL, TO-THE-POINT AND IN-THE-MOMENT."

- The Northeast Avalon Times

The Coral Beach Casefiles series by Matthew LeDrew:

For more information, please visit

www.engenbooks.com

ENGEN

BOOKS

ABOUT THE AUTHOR

Brad Dunne is a freelance writer and editor from St. John's, Newfoundland. He began his writing career as an intern at *The Walrus* magazine and has published journalism and essays in publications such as *Maisonneuve*, *The Canadian Encyclopedia*, and *Herizons*. His short fiction has been featured in *In/Words*, *Acta Victoriana*, *Pulp Science-Fiction from the Rock*, *Terror Nova*, and, *The Cuffer Anthology*.

In October 2018 he released his first novel, *After Dark Vapours*.

He maintains a blog at braddunne.ca. He's also active on twitter (@braddunne1796) and instagram (@yoloflaherty).